COLTON

SEALs of Honor, Book 23

Dale Mayer

COLTON: SEALS OF HONOR, BOOK 23
Dale Mayer
Valley Publishing

Copyright © 2020

ISBN-13: 978-1-773363-43-1
Print Edition

Books in This Series:

About This Book

His next flight becomes a fight for his life ... and the life of the two pilots.

Colton is helping out on a training session in Greenland, currently in midair. The copilot is a woman he knew intimately and had planned to reconnect with, only life never seemed to give him that window. His flight turns into a nightmare as the engine blows, and he, along with the two pilots, are forced to abandon the bird and jump into the Arctic Ocean.

Kate Winnows might not have been overjoyed to see Colton as her only passenger, but she's darn happy he's here when all hell breaks loose. She'd never forgotten him. Had hoped to reconnect but, like him, her life was busy, finding each of them all over the planet. Now she needs him to help her save her reputation, her job and possibly her life ... again. And, if she can make it happen, she wants a second chance to show him what he means to her.

Especially when they find out the crash was no accident but just the tip of the iceberg in a case involving blackmail, drugs and ... murder.

Sign up to be notified of all Dale's releases here!

http://smarturl.it/dmnewsletter

COMPLIMENTARY DOWNLOAD

DOWNLOAD a *__complimentary__* copy of TUESDAY'S CHILD? Just tell me where to send it!

http://dalemayer.com/starterlibrarytc/

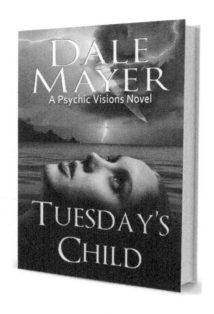

PROLOGUE

COLTON EDGEWOOD BOARDED the military plane at Coronado, on the first leg of his journey overseas to the Thule Air Base in Greenland. He was okay with that, but, at the same time, he hadn't been home long enough to really get his feet under him. And, after helping Taylor these last few days, it seemed like such a rush job. Colton had really planned on staying on base for a week at least.

He'd served in a unique position in Afghanistan—as a liaison for one of the joint military teams, pulling together group training of "friendly" wars, all in a mission to foster peace and to further everybody's education and skills. So now he was headed to Greenland for a similar operation.

Greenland was a strategic site for the Thule Air Base. He didn't expect to be there for too long and would head off to Africa afterward, at least as far as he understood. For now. His orders were never firm for long. He'd get one step on a journey but would never quite know where he would go from there.

Still, he'd never been to Greenland and was looking forward to it. With a population of fewer than sixty thousand on the whole island, it was a unique corner of the world, where nobody owned their own land. Instead buyers were granted the right to use it, and everybody worked together to make their society the way they wanted it. The population was mostly native people, and Colton really appreciated the different viewpoint they brought.

He shifted position. He was the only one on this military flight, along with a ton of cargo. He wished he could have ridden in the cockpit, but, with room only for a pilot and a copilot, Colton definitely wasn't small enough to squeeze between them up there. The trip was long but uneventful.

Just as they prepared for a landing, he heard a large explosion on the left side of the plane. He bolted from his seat and stuck his head in the cockpit to take a look in that direction. The left engine was on fire. He swore.

The copilot glanced at him and said, "Take your seat."

He nodded but grabbed three parachutes instead, in case they had to abandon the plane. He made his way forward again to see the pilots calm and controlled but issuing updates to the base as they approached. "I've got two extra parachutes here, in case you guys need them."

The copilot nodded. "Hopefully not," she said.

Kate. Kate Winnows. Somebody he'd known for many years, had flown with a couple times and once had shared an overnight stay. That had been a hot and heavy night—then they had both showered the next morning and carried on with their individual lives. But to see her here and now just put another human face on this. He didn't recognize the pilot.

Kate looked at him again and said, "Take your seat, Colton."

At that, he nodded, grabbed his parachute and fastened it on, then took a seat. He couldn't buckle in with the chute on, but he wasn't letting go of it. At the moment, the parachute seemed more critical than the seat belt.

The plane careened to the side and slipped downward at

a rate that was more than a little nauseating. He caught his breath, following the safety procedures he knew they would go through now. He had been in similar situations before. Not exactly this but ... He leaned forward to look out the cockpit window, hoping to see land in the distance. Regardless, if the pilots had put out a Mayday call, they could now jump and get free and clear of the plane, if headed for a crash.

Kate joined him in the cargo bay, holding onto a nearby strap, and said in a curt but controlled tone, "We have to bail."

"Understood." When he rose, he immediately fell as the plane listed again to the side. "What about the pilot?" he yelled over the loud din, scrambling to his feet once more.

"He's coming," she said, righting herself as well. She grabbed her parachute, and he helped her strap it on.

The two made their way to the cockpit, where the pilot still tried to guide the plane. She called out to him, "George, come on. We're done."

He nodded. "I know," he said. "I just wanted to make sure we got out to the ocean, where this doesn't come down on anybody." Finally he bolted toward them and, with their help, got buckled into his parachute. He looked around the plane and said, "It won't be that easy to get out of here. It'll be hard to get clear of the plane."

"I know," Colton said, as he struggled against the downward angle of the plane to reach the emergency door, kicked it open and basically tossed Kate out.

The pilot raised his eyebrows and shook his head. "Damn, this is the first time for me."

He didn't get a chance to say more because Colton already had pushed the pilot outside in the frigid air. Colton jumped out behind them. Colton watched as the plane dove, flames shooting out behind it, as it beelined for the deep dark ocean below.

They'd gone from an ugly and dangerous situation to an uglier and deadlier one.

Nothing was easy about landing in the Arctic Ocean. Hypothermia would set in within ten to twelve minutes. After that? Then it wouldn't matter who came to rescue them—it would already be too late.

CHAPTER 1

COLTON PULLED HIS cord and watched his parachute billow above him, tugging him upward with a sudden jolt that gave him a better view of the other two. Kate appeared to be fine, but George struggled. It looked like his first chute didn't deploy.

"Pull the second one! Pull the second one!" Colton shouted. The pilot did, and, thank God, that one deployed.

With the three of them now drifting toward the ocean below, the plane careened off to the side and hit the hard surface of the ocean full-on, exploding on impact, sending fire and metal parts everywhere. Soon it was just wreckage burning on the surface of the ocean. Kate was still a ways away.

Colton shifted to direct his descent toward her, so he could keep an eye on the two of them below him. Part of the problem with a chute was the fact you had to get rid of it once you hit the water. The chutes were heavy and could pull you down easily. He could see ships coming toward them already, which was good, but now he and the pilots had to stay alive long enough for the rescuers to reach them.

The trio had avoided the plane crash but were still ill prepared for the icy water waiting for them. More than that, the parachute lines were even more dangerous than the parachute itself once in the water, it was easy to get tangled up in the lines and drown. Colton would ditch his chute as soon as he got close enough to jump into the water because he hated the dangers inherent in those lines. Plus he had to be free and clear to help the pilots. Yet he had to time the cutting of his lines just right. He didn't want to do that too soon, extending his time in the frigid water. Yet he had to cut his lines at the last possible moment before he hit the water. But then, he'd done this many, many times. He wasn't so sure about the other two.

They were military, but not navy, and water was his element, not necessarily theirs. Ever since he was a kid, he'd wanted to be a Navy SEAL, and achieving that status had been a crowning glory in his life. Absolutely nothing had the same sense of achievement since then.

But he knew the dangers of this crash-landing. As long as the rescue boats moved toward them, they wouldn't be in the freezing water for too long. Judging the distance of the boats coming toward them, he realized their arrival would cut it close to that ten-to-twelve-minute hypothermia mark.

He maneuvered his position so he was between Kate and George. George looked to be less comfortable up here in the air, whereas Kate hung on like a trooper, studying the water below. Colton was less worried about any sea life in the ocean than the actual temperature of the water itself. They were also heavily geared up, and the work boots they wore would feel like fifty pounds by the time they soaked up water.

Just ten feet above the water he quickly unbuckled his chute and dropped it. Kate had hit the surface on his left, and George had splashed down on his right. He was in between them. Closing his legs, he slammed into the water and kicked hard to resurface.

Breaking through the ocean, he checked on the others. George was closest and still struggling. Colton headed toward him first. "Stay calm. I'll cut your lines." With his knife, Colton cut the buckles, pulling the lines away. "Can you swim?"

George nodded. "Just not well."

"Try to float," Colton said. "I've got to get Kate." And he headed to where Kate was, trying to undo her buckles. Once everything got soaking wet, it was that much harder to maneuver. He knew her fingers would start to freeze soon, faster if she panicked.

He called out to her, "I'm here. Calm down. Control the panic."

She took several deep breaths, and he could see the fear in her eyes as she looked at him. "Tread water gently," he said. "I'll cut you free."

Then he quickly got her buckles cut and helped her get out of the harness. "Can you swim?"

She nodded and started to strike out hard.

"Don't swim too hard or too fast," he said. "You'll burn up your energy. Hypothermia is our demon to beat."

She shot him a look.

George still struggled. Colton's SEALs training kicked in, and he put George into an assisted floating position. With Kate at his side, he told George, "Stay strong. The boats are coming."

George's teeth were already chattering. "I didn't expect to go out like this."

"You're *not* going out like this," Colton said fiercely. "*Fight.* We just have to stay afloat until they get here."

They floated, looped together, trying to preserve their strength and heat.

"What happened to the plane that caused the fire?" Colton asked after a moment.

Kate shook her head. "Explosion in the left engine. None of our diagnostics gave a reason. It was all fine, and then it wasn't."

"A bomb?" he asked.

"Possibly," George said, "but it easily could have been a damaged fuel line. I don't know. But something caused it to explode, and now nothing will be left for the military to discern what happened."

"Sounds like you guys have enemies," Colton joked.

"Yes," George said, his teeth still chattering.

Colton hated to say it, but George wasn't doing well. "George, you have to hang on. The boats will be here in a few minutes. Tell me about this enemy you're talking about."

"I'm supposed to testify against two coworkers—two pilots," he said. "They were smuggling drugs."

Colton's breath gushed out in a *whoosh*. "Wow," he said. "Didn't see that coming."

"Yeah, I know," George whispered.

Colton looked over at Kate to see a hard look in her eyes. "Did you know about it?"

She nodded. "Yes. Both men have been removed from active duty and are awaiting trial."

"Of course they are," Colton said. "Court-martialed and the military police are involved, right?"

"Yes, on both counts," she said. "The military trial isn't for another four months though."

"Right, and, if they can get rid of George, then, of course, they walk free."

"Exactly," George said. "And I've got a sorry-ass feeling

they'll be right about that."

"Do you want to see them walk free?" Colton asked, as he tried to keep George floating and fighting for his life, while Colton kept an eye on Kate. "I can hear the boats, George. Stay calm." But George wasn't answering. Colton gave him a shake and smacked him hard on the cheek.

George groaned.

"Did you hear me, George?"

"I don't want to hear you," he said. "I'm so cold."

"Soldier, buck up!" Colton snapped. "That's an order."

George's eyes flew open, and he stared up at the blue sky. "One of these days those orders can't be followed."

"It won't be today, dammit," Colton roared. "Stay awake, soldier. You can hear the boats. They're here." He twisted George's head so he could see the approaching cruiser.

"Oh, wow," George said. "You were serious."

"I saw them up above," Colton said, "but we still have to get somebody from the cruiser to us." Colton looked over at Kate. She was desperate to hang on but fading.

Nobody could keep this up for long, so Colton knew it would be close. "If you can't stay on the surface," he said to her, "you let me know."

She just glared at him. "Like hell," she said. "George needs to be rescued so those two assholes who did this don't get away with it."

"Are they the kind of assholes who would do this?" Colton asked.

"Who knows? But, if this was sabotage, George is likely the target."

"What about you?" Colton asked. "Do you have any enemies?"

"Not that I know of."

George gave a broken laugh. "Your ex-boyfriend would do this, Kate. Remember? He said he would make sure you paid."

"It was one of the reasons why I was okay to fly with you," she said, a weak attempt at a joke. "We were both targeted."

Colton swore. "How come I didn't get any warning to not fly with either of you?"

"Because you were tossed on at the last minute," she said, "but it's not like we could have warned you anyway. But I'm sorry you're involved."

"I'm not involved, but I am caught up in it. And I'll be damned if I'll let either of you die. We have a rescue right here, right now." He could see men getting into a Zodiac. "Come on. They're in the Zodiac. We've got minutes to go. That's it."

"Too late," George said, his voice slurred. "So cold. C-Can't feel anything."

"You'll feel it all soon enough," Colton said urgently. "It'll hurt like shit when the blood starts moving back through your body."

"Maybe it's better this way," George murmured, his eyes falling shut again. Colton reached over and smacked him hard. George groaned again but didn't open his eyes.

Colton looked over at Kate.

"Don't waste the energy on me," she said. "I'm still here."

But she was failing. He could see it. Her feet and arms were moving much slower, and her body was sinking, then popping back up again. He knew that, somewhere in the next few moments, she would go down and not pop back up again. He could hold out for another five or ten minutes, maybe fifteen, but that would be his max too.

As good as he was, and he knew what he could do, the temperature here would slowly sap away his own strength. He hadn't come prepared for an Arctic Ocean mission. Not one out in the freezing cold water itself. He was doing everything he could to preserve his own body heat, but he expended some of his energy to keep George afloat. Colton caught George slipping under again and smacked him hard once more. "We're almost there. Hang on, George."

But George was past responding.

Shit! Colton was using the standard rescue position to keep George floating beside him, but, as he watched, Kate went under and didn't come back up. He reached down with his boot and tossed her higher up in the water and grabbed her by the back of her jacket. He yelled for help. He could hear their rescuers coming, and so Colton started moving toward them as quickly as possible but still in control. Slow and steady won the race, but Mother Nature could be a bitch, and she always tried to trump everything else.

Sometimes humanity won too.

Suddenly the Zodiac was here, and hands reached for him. He passed up George first because that was the side they were on, then moved to get Kate up. Afterward, as he tried to pull himself up into the Zodiac, he could feel the slow effect of the cold as his legs didn't want to work and his hands fumbled. Willing arms caught him and yanked him aboard, dumping him into the bottom of the boat.

"Perfect timing, guys," he said, his teeth chattering. "Perfect timing." Colton stared up at the sky. "But it would have been really nice if you'd gotten here about five minutes earlier."

He could hear the men shouting orders as they raced toward the cruiser. George was unloaded first, and then Kate was carried up next, conscious but shivering badly. Colton had taken a few minutes to pump some oxygen through his body, but his body was cold, and he knew it needed to reheat fast. One of the men reached down, grabbed him by the shoulder and helped him to his feet. He stumbled forward.

"You okay, soldier?"

"Always," he said, right before he collapsed to the deck.

KATE WINNOWS WOKE up and stared around the small room. Everything was white, and she lay on a medical bed, yet the room seemed to rock. *I must still be on the destroyer.* The memories came crushing back, causing her to shudder. The plane went down, and the water had been so damn cold. Of everything that had to be the worst. Sure, she had an initial panic, knowing the plane was going down, but realizing they had the chutes gave her a course of action to focus on.

Once she was buckled in to her chute, it was a matter of getting George strapped up and deplaning. Floating down was an experience like nothing she remembered. She'd done parachute training, but it was always under calm conditions. Never like this. She knew, in theory, what landing in the ocean would be like, but she wasn't prepared for how quickly the ocean zapped the heat from her bones and the blood from her vessels, leaving her body as a block of ice, like the glaciers all around them.

She knew that, if it hadn't been for Colton, neither she nor George would have survived. At that, she sat up and looked around. She saw several other beds, but only one was occupied, where two men were working on that patient.

George. "Is he okay?"

One of the men walked to her, checking her temperature. "He's dealing with severe hypothermia," the doctor said. "We're treating him. You are suffering from hypothermia yourself, so let's keep your movements to a minimum, please."

She noted she had been wrapped up in special blankets, and her body, although it should have been warm, was not. "I'm still so cold," she whispered, and almost immediately her body started to shiver. "Colton?" she asked.

"He's fine," the doctor said. "He's probably in the mess hall, tanking up on hot coffee right now."

"I wish I was there," she muttered, her teeth chattering.

The man tucked yet another warm blanket around her. "Give yourself a chance to warm up," he said, then went back to George's side.

Kate knew from their discussions that it was not good news for George. He was suffering a lot more than she was. When the doctor finally returned to her again, she said, "The plane was sabotaged."

His gaze sharpened. "Does Colton know?"

"Yes," she said. "He does."

"Then trust us to look after it," he said.

"I'm worried George won't make it. And that whoever did this will have succeeded in killing him."

"We're working on it," the doctor said quietly. "You have to look after yourself. We can't have two of you not making it." And, with that, Kate's heart sank, as she realized just how bad George's situation was. He was a family man, who had come to marriage late in life, and now had three teenage boys. They needed him. He must keep fighting.

Mentally she sent out a message. *Come on, George. Fight. Colton kept you alive out there. I need you to stay alive in here.*

Even if he lost some fingers or toes, he had to stay alive. Even minus his legs, his sons still needed him. And, with that thought, she turned to her own healing, telling her body to warm up fast. She wanted to see whoever had done this to them soon caught so they would pay for their crimes. And finally, to Colton, she sent out a message, whispering, "Thank you, love."

She'd always known he was honorable. And that one night they'd come together in a heated flash had been nothing like she'd ever experienced before. She didn't even really understand who he was at first. But when she realized he was one of Mason's SEALs, she'd shaken her head and had stepped back. At the time she hadn't been interested in permanency.

Obviously he hadn't been either because he had walked away with nothing but a wave and a smile. Just another ship in the night. She didn't know if he'd felt the same crash and burn when they made love that she had or not—all her senses had been fired up, almost like a homecoming. But, when he left, it turned out to be a rude awakening, as she could never forget him.

She had heard about him every once in a while, that he'd been rising up the ranks, but they hadn't crossed paths until today. And this was something she desperately wished hadn't happened. Who needed this kind of crap?

After a life-and-death event like this one, it had Kate thinking. She had already been looking to settle down lately. Yet she hadn't found that special someone, at least not in a permanent way. Only in the last couple years did it really bother her, as she saw others having families. But not her.

She never had a relationship last long enough. She thought it was her fault mostly. Part of it was her circumstances as a navy pilot. She was here, then she was gone; she was there, and then she was gone. This type of job didn't foster permanency.

Those who had come into the military with a stable relationship seemed to go home to them. She hadn't had that. She had a vagabond aspect to her life that she probably couldn't change until she either transferred stateside or decided to ground herself—because the competition for pilots in places like Coronado was huge. And she didn't have the same seniority others did.

Or maybe she needed to change divisions and do something else. Maybe work in the private sector as a commercial pilot. She'd certainly been tempted to do that. She'd had offers she was reconsidering now, since she had about three months left on her current contract. Now if only she could figure out what she wanted to do after that.

CHAPTER 2

AFTER WHAT SEEMED like a long sleep, Kate woke up to find Colton standing at the end of her hospital bed. She started. "Wow," she said. "What a way to wake up."

"You okay?" he asked, grabbing a chair, spinning it around and sitting on it backward. He always had that easy grace she loved.

"I'm alive," she said. "How's George?"

"Stable, but in serious condition. He's no longer here. They airlifted him to the base hospital a few hours ago. They have better facilities for him."

Her eyebrows shot up. "I didn't even wake up," she wailed. "I wanted to say goodbye."

"Let's hope you get a chance to say hello instead," he said with a gentle smile.

She winced at that. "I gather he's in pretty rough shape still?"

"He is," Colton said. "How are you doing?"

"I've been better, but I'm not as cold anymore."

"The doc will check you over again, but I wanted to sneak in beforehand."

"Why?" she asked.

"I wanted as many details as you could give me. I want to make sure we find out who did this."

"You won't be allowed to do anything about it. You

know the military police will be handling it."

"Yep," he said, "I know that. But I also know Mason's team was brought in on several special investigations. Nobody knows about it, but it's been happening for the last year or so."

"I heard rumors too," she said, "but I don't always have access to the same info you guys get."

"I hear you," he said. "You're a hell of a pilot, and I appreciate you keeping me alive up there."

She snorted. "Not sure about being a hell of a pilot. George was at the controls there at the end."

"Nicely done by both of you, but I don't leave alone," Colton said. "I make sure everybody goes with me."

"Yeah, I seem to recall you pitching me from the plane."

"Oh, come on. I—"

She laughed. "Well, George's still alive, and so am I because of you, so thanks."

"Ditto." The two of them just stared at each other, neither mentioning their past. She was unsure how to even bring it up or if she should just move on from it.

Finally Colton asked, "How have you been?"

She shrugged. "Not too bad. And you?" She hated the stilted semiformal tone to their voices.

He cracked a smile. "Never better. Life has been really busy. I just came back from months in Afghanistan. I was hoping to stay in Coronado for a while, but I was asked to go to Greenland to impart some tips and tricks for a training session here," he said with a wry smile.

"So you weren't supposed to be here long?"

"No. Some training here, then to Africa."

"Ah," she said. "I heard you were doing a lot more training these days."

"Yeah, it's definitely shifting my world."

"But you're still an active SEAL?"

"Yes." He tilted his head in a nod, but she could see his eyes studying her, checking her color and making sure she was moving and awake. She shifted in the bed and groaned. "So, how come, even though we didn't hit anything, I feel like my body just got run over by a semi-truck?"

"But you did hit something. You hit the great big ocean. But some of that physical pain is due to the exhaustion from the extreme cold," Colton said. "There's nothing quite like it. It'll take time to recover."

"It feels like I'll never recover," Kate said, collapsing back down again.

"How about some hot drinks?"

"I feel like they damn-near funneled that stuff right into my stomach," she said, "and bypassed my throat."

At that, he burst out laughing. "How about I get you some warm coffee? We'll see if you can drink that."

"Sounds good," she said. And she closed her eyes as he got up and left.

KATE HADN'T LOOKED too bad, which was a blessing because he'd had a look at George, who hadn't looked great. The doctors had high hopes for him to recover, but they weren't sure if he would end up with all his fingers and toes and potentially even his limbs. However, Colton didn't want to look at those problems until necessary. At the moment, he was all about making sure Kate was as good as she could be. Because he needed to know everything she could tell him. He'd wanted to get details, but it was obvious she wasn't doing as well as she could, and he didn't want to impact her healing by revisiting the crash and stirring up unpleasant memories.

He headed into the cafeteria area, picked up two coffees, adding cream and a little bit of sugar to the one for her—it was the way she used to take it—and he knew the sugar wouldn't be a bad thing right now, given her condition. Then he saw fresh muffins. He plated four, added several pats of butter, and, with two knives in his hand, he carried the plate on top of one of the cups and made his way back to the sick bay.

The doctor sitting at a desk to the side looked up and smiled as Colton walked in. "Hopefully some sugar is in that coffee," he said.

Colton nodded and said, "There's a little, but I can get more if need be."

"No," Kate said, "a little is fine."

The doctor helped her raise the upper half of her bed, and, when he stepped back, Colton asked, "How is she?"

"A very lucky lady," he said. "She cheated death twice, both times barely beating it."

"Isn't that the truth?" she murmured. "I'll take barely beating death any day over the alternative." She looked at Colton. "And I owe one of them to you."

"Well, I owe one of them to you, so we're even," Colton said, as he moved a small table beside her and swung it around so it was over her lap. "Here. Get some of this down."

"I wonder how long I'll be cold for," she muttered, hugging the cup.

"Hours, if not days," the doctor said. "Hypothermia, for all that we know about it, can present as different symptoms in different people."

"Interesting," she murmured. "I guess you don't have all that many cases to study."

"Exactly," he said. "At least not severe cases who survived." With that, he gave her a smile and headed off.

Colton sat down at the edge of the bed and said, "Did he give you a free pass?"

"You heard him. I'm doing okay. As long as that continues, I can leave soon."

"We can hope so," Colton said, studying her color. She looked so much better.

"Well, they know we survived, I presume."

"Yes," he said, and then he lowered his voice. "But we haven't spread the word as to what happened."

"Why is that?" she asked.

"Because somebody tried to kill us. We don't want whoever it was to know they didn't succeed. The news is that the plane went down, but not a whole lot has been shared otherwise."

"Great," she said. "I hadn't really considered that." She took a sip of her coffee, wincing as the hot brew hit her throat.

He watched when she settled back. Now she had even more color and a brighter smile. It was her smile that had caught his attention when he had first met her. They'd been an inferno together, and he'd basked in that fire willingly. He'd left the following morning, fully planning on calling her, but his next mission had him gone for months that time. And then his opportunity to reconnect in a timely fashion was gone.

When she didn't take more sips of her coffee, he asked, "Is it too hot?"

"No. It's fine," she said. "It's just that everything is so

sensitive. My lips, tongue, ... fingers." She wiggled them at him playfully.

"They will be for a while," he said. "We are being airlifted out today," he said. "We'll leave the destroyer in a few hours. The question is whether you need to go to a specialized medical facility from here or if you will be fine to walk off on your own."

"I'll walk," she said, "but I don't know where my clothes went."

"I'll see what I can find for you." Colton stood and took a sip of coffee. "How many of those muffins will you eat?"

"If you sit down in that chair," she said, "we could share them."

He hesitated.

"Come on. Clothing will wait," she said, "unless you're telling me that we're flying out right now?"

"No," he said. "Not for a few hours yet."

"Then let's eat. I'm starved."

CHAPTER 3

A FTER COLTON LEFT and returned just long enough to drop off a set of clothing for her, Kate got up slowly, her body shaky and weak. Once she was dressed, she made her way to the facilities and back, sitting on her hospital bed again. She hated to say it, but the cold had taken more from her than she had realized. Plus the rocking movement of the destroyer didn't help her balance any.

When the doctor returned once more, he smiled to see her dressed. "Well, that's a good sign."

She nodded. "I just wasn't expecting to feel quite so weak."

"Your body has taken a huge hit. It's amazing that it can even recover so fast from the stresses you went through. But, in another day or two, I think you'll be right as rain."

"Any update on George?"

"He's still alive," the doctor said cheerfully. "It'll be a few days yet."

She nodded sadly. "Well, let's hope he makes it. He's got three teenage boys, and they need their dad."

The doctor's face sobered. "That they do."

Looking around, she said, "I know Colton is heading out soon, and I was hoping to go with him."

"You can. In about two hours," he said, "so you might as well sit back and relax. We'll have to see if we've got some boots for you."

She looked down at the socks on her feet and smiled. "Did everything get cut off of us?"

He nodded. "Not your boots, but I don't know that we'll get them dry in time."

She nodded, saying, "Even if they're wet, at least they fit."

"I've got people working on it," he said. "We did have to cut everything else off though. Sorry."

"Understood," she said. "I've got on layers of clothing now, so that's at least something." When she shivered again, she shifted back onto the bed and pulled the blanket up around her. "Such a weird feeling," she murmured sleepily.

"Just rest. You'll be out of here in no time." And, with that, the doctor turned and disappeared.

She fell into a light dozing nap, surfacing and waking, going back under again. But, when she woke the next time, she saw her boots sitting beside her. They were partially dry, though not completely, but efforts were ongoing to soak up the moisture. Newspaper had been stuffed inside to absorb a little more too. As she sat up slowly and reached for them, Colton came in.

"Perfect," he said. "I was figuring out what to do about your footwear."

"They cut off everything else," she said, "but apparently not these."

"Which is a good thing," he said. "If they're anything like mine, they'll feel like they're superheavy, unless they're completely dry." He picked them up, pulled out the newspaper and shook his head. "Nope, they sure aren't."

"But they do fit," she said, "so it is what it is."

"Agreed." He waited while she tied up her boots.

Then she looked at him and said, "I gather we're leaving now?"

"We sure are," he said.

Once her boots were tied, she stood. She was still a little woozy, and, with his arms half supporting her, she took several steps forward.

"Let me try walking on my own, see if I can get my sea legs back," she said, then walked around the small room carefully. She smiled and said, "I should be good." The trouble was, she didn't have a jacket, and she was still cold. As if reading her thoughts, Colton said, "My clothes weren't cut off of me, and I was able to get them into a dryer." He took off his jacket and slung it around her shoulders.

She snuggled into the warmth and stopped, closing her eyes. "Wow," she said. "What a difference."

"Remember. You'll feel cold for a while." Snagging her arm, he tucked it in against his elbow. "Come on. Let's go."

She followed him down the ramp and upstairs to the deck of the destroyer. There they stood in the shadows until given clearance. Finally they boarded the helicopter, he behind her, checking on her every move. When she finally sagged into her seat and buckled up, she sighed with relief. "Never would I have thought getting cold like that would have such a debilitating effect for so long."

"Just goes to show you," he said, "how bad it really was."

As soon as the helicopter took off, Kate studied the ocean around them. "Are we still going to the same air base?"

"Yep," he said cheerfully.

Thirty-five minutes later they hovered over the airstrip. "I'm not even sure what I'm supposed to do now. I was heading to the last leg of my flight," she said. "I thought I was taking a flight back to Coronado, but now I'm not sure."

"You need a couple days off," Colton said confidently. "So don't let them send you out just yet."

"I know. Maybe that's why I'm supposed to report to the doctor when I land."

"You came out of the medical bay on the ship," he said. "Standard practice."

When they did land, they were greeted by a team. Kate was separated from Colton and led into another medical bay, where she was checked over and told she was on a forty-eight-hour furlough for medical reasons. She nodded and asked, "Where am I staying?"

One of the men smiled and said, "I'll take you over."

She followed him to some barracks, where she was given a small room to herself. She immediately stretched out on the bed and closed her eyes. She should have asked where Colton was but was so damn tired that she couldn't keep her eyes open, so she didn't fight it.

A knock came on her door sometime later and woke her. "Come in," she called out.

Colton stepped in. "Have you debriefed yet?"

She shook her head. "But, of course, I've got that to do too, don't I?" She groaned and sat up.

"The sooner, the better."

She looked up at him. "Have you?"

"I've just come from there."

She nodded and said, "Better to do it now, if I can."

"That's why I came to get you. I wanted to make sure we got it done as soon as possible. Then it's over, and you can rest." He held out a hand.

Smiling, she placed hers in it.

IT WAS HARD for Colton to not feel the electricity every time he touched her. Even though she still felt sick and was obviously weak, something about this woman stirred his senses like no other. He'd left that morning way back when because that was how he thought she'd wanted it. That was how they'd arranged it, an unspoken agreement—two ships in the night and then carry on. He'd lost track of her for a long time after that.

Then he heard stories. Every once in a while he'd hear her name mentioned, which would bring it all back again. He hadn't realized she was piloting the plane he was on until he'd gone up front. He wondered when she hopped on because he didn't think she'd been there in Coronado. He'd have to ask her, but right now they were approaching the investigators.

Colton had been asked what condition she was in, and he'd volunteered to see if she was willing to do this now. It was obviously better for everyone if they could debrief now and get as much information as possible in the hands of the investigators. Colton pulled up a chair for her and helped her sit down. He knew she wasn't that weak, but it wouldn't hurt for the investigators to understand she was still recovering.

With that, the interview got started. She answered all the questions honestly, at least Colton thought so, if he was any good at reading body language. She had no idea what had happened, just that the left engine blew up without warning. She did explain about her ex-boyfriend and about George's legal case.

By the time they were done, Colton hadn't learned anything new, and that was frustrating. He had hoped she would have picked up something. Then the questions started in his direction again. *Had he seen anything before he boarded in Coronado? Had he seen anyone unauthorized around the plane?* He shook his head. He turned to look at her.

"You didn't board at Coronado, did you?"

She shook her head. "No, Halifax. I was on layover and joined George there."

He nodded. "And, no," he said, as he turned to face the others. "I didn't see anything on that layover either."

"We already asked the Canadian government to take a look at their video cameras," one of the investigators said in frustration. "We do have a good rapport with them, and they sent them right over, but, so far we haven't picked up anybody or anything suspicious on them."

"Several other soldiers were there," Colton said. "Two other American planes were at the base."

"Yes. One ran into trouble and was flying with the second, so both landed," he said. "But that was a different story entirely."

"Maybe," Colton said, "but it was opportunity, if someone was looking for one."

"For one of the other soldiers on the other flights?"

"If this was on purpose, then, yeah," Colton said.

"It's not like the passengers on the other flights would have known they were landing at Gander International Airport," he said.

"No, but it's a normal flight path," he said, "so was always a possibility."

"I hope you're not saying the other plane that ran into some trouble was also sabotaged?"

"No," Colton said. "I mean, it's possible obviously, but that would be taking a big risk."

"If you think about it," Kate said, "it expands the suspect

pool."

The men facing them stared at her.

She shrugged. "Well, just think about it. Now you have to consider all those people."

"Do the video cameras cover all the angles all the time?" Colton asked.

The men shook their heads. "No, but their camera system is good, and it would have been similar to ours," one said. "And we all know that, if somebody wanted something to happen, it's not out of the realm of possibility."

"Unfortunately it's all too possible," Colton said. He looked over to see Kate's color fading quickly. "Gentlemen, I think that needs to be all for the day. We can come back tomorrow, if needed."

The men nodded, and Colton reached out a hand to Kate.

She looked at him gratefully, then addressed the investigators. "I'm more than happy to answer more questions," she said, "I just don't know what else I can tell you."

"If we have more questions, we'll get in touch with you tomorrow. You'll be at least two days recovering, and then I understand you're heading back stateside when you can, right?"

"Yes," she said.

"So you're here forty-eight hours anyway and grounded indefinitely, until we get to the bottom of this. It's nothing personal. We just need to have you available for questioning."

CHAPTER 4

KATE TOOK IT like a sock to her gut, but she rallied and smiled at them. "Let's hope we get a fast answer to all this," and, with a salute, she turned, and Colton led her back outside again.

"Wow," she said. "I didn't expect to be grounded."

"I think it's twofold on their part. Not only were you part of the sabotage plot," he said, "but, if you fly again, and somebody is targeting you, then whoever goes on your flight is also potentially in danger."

She stared up at him, her eyes filled with pain. "That's not what I wanted to think about," she snapped. But he just smiled at her, as if waiting for her to come around. She sighed. "Okay, fine, so it makes logical sense. I just don't like it."

"None of us ever do," he said. "Now, before you crash for the night, how about some food?"

"That would be good," she said. "That muffin was tasty, but it wasn't enough."

"It was two muffins," he said, "and I'm pretty sure you ate part of my second one too."

"Who's counting?" she said with an airy wave of her hand. "But, if we can get some food, that would be good." She shrugged and said, "I don't even know what time it is here."

"It's coming on dinner," Colton said, "so let's head there first."

"I need to figure out where my room is," Kate said, turning in confusion. "I'm lost."

"I'll take you back afterward."

She looked at him. "You'll be here for the next few days too, won't you?"

"Yeah, it seems like my plans might have changed."

"You're not heading off again?"

"No," he said just as cheerfully as before, with almost too much enthusiasm. "I'm grounded as well."

"I'm sorry," she murmured. "It's been a shit day all around."

Inside the mess tent they each picked up a tray and walked down the aisle of food. There was lots of it, and it was all hot. Kate didn't recognize many of the dishes, but she was happy to take whatever was offered. She could hear Colton asking for beef and gravy and getting her plate filled so it was heaping. She stared at it and looked at him sideways.

"Remember the muffins?" he said in a low voice. "Sometimes you come out of a trauma like that without any appetite at all, and sometimes you come out of that extreme-cold situation, feeling like you're starving and can't get full."

"Well, as I first looked at this, I was thinking it was way too much," she said, "but now I'm wondering if it's enough."

"We're not done yet either," Colton said and moved her along, where he served her a hot bowl of soup. "Let's go sit over there."

With their trays set down, she sat carefully and took everything off her tray. Colton took it from her and smiled.

"I'll be back in a minute," he said, then disappeared, only to return with water and more coffee.

She smiled at that. "Do you always treat people so nicely?"

"Always," he said. "It doesn't cost anything to be kind."

"True," she said, feeling bad because, of course, she'd been teasing him, but he really was being very helpful in looking after her. When they were both seated, she started in on the soup and stopped to savor the first spoonful. "Wow, this is really good."

"The soup will help warm you up faster than anything," Colton said. "I can see you're still cold."

Kate looked down at her fingers, still on the verge of trembling. "My body still needs a couple days, right?"

"Definitely a couple days," he agreed.

By the time Kate had finished her soup and had started in on her plate, she began to feel a little better, but, when halfway through, she felt her energy waning. She kept eating, but it was more of an effort. When she finally stopped, she just looked at Colton.

"Let's go," he said. "Let's get you back to bed before you can't walk anymore."

"Too late," she said, standing and wavering on her feet. He gripped her arm and wrapped it around his waist and then wrapped an arm around her. Carefully he moved her through the cafeteria, and she knew when a silence fell around them that they were being watched. "I'm sorry. I'm making a spectacle of myself."

"Don't you worry," he said. "They probably all know what we've survived, and those who didn't now will."

"Yeah, but how come I'm so weak and not you?" she grumbled. He chuckled, the sound lovely against her ear.

"It's not that it's you or me," he said. "We're both survivors. Latch on to that and don't forget it. Everybody here isn't thinking about what kind of shape we're in. Every one of them is damn grateful they weren't in our position."

She smiled at that. "If you say so." But she could see that, if she had been here watching someone else in her situation, she would be feeling very sympathetic and also grateful it hadn't been her. Back in her small room, Colton opened the door and helped her so she could collapse on the bed.

"I don't want you sleeping in your clothes like that," he warned.

"What difference does it make? Sleep is sleep," she muttered, collapsing on her back and staying there.

"No," he said. "It isn't. You really need to get restorative sleep. You need to be comfortable, so you can get the best sleep you can."

"I couldn't possibly *not* sleep if I tried," she said. "You have no idea how exhausted I am."

"Actually I do," he said, "and so I still worry. At least let's get those boots off you—and the pants." And, true to his words, he had her boots unbuckled and pulled off in no time.

She said, "I need the socks on though."

"No way, they're wet from the boots."

She managed to sit up again and said, "You'll have to leave."

He grinned and said, "You don't have anything I haven't seen."

"Maybe," she said with a tiny smile, "but it doesn't feel the same."

"No," he said, "it's not at all the same. But you're being

foolish because what you need to be is tucked under that blanket right now, so shuck those pants and get that shirt off. I'll turn my back."

She stripped down quickly, before dashing under the covers.

"Damn it, your lips are turning blue." Swearing, Colton grabbed another blanket from the cupboard and placed it on top of her. "Do you need another one?" he asked, and she could feel the worry in his tone and the waves of concern emanating from him.

She shook her head, trying to stop her teeth from chattering. "I should be good," she said. "I just need to sleep."

"But will you?" he asked.

"I'll be fine," she said. "Go get some rest. I'll be okay."

"I'm only two doors down, if you run into trouble."

"What kind of trouble can I be getting into? I'll just be lying here, sleeping."

"Don't lock the door, please," he said. "I'll come in and check on you."

"Okay, good for you. I'm sure I'll be snoring, so don't wake me up." On that note, she closed her eyes, and, as her body trembled, she sank deeper into the covers. Once she heard the door shut behind him, she let out a deep sigh and let sleep overtake her.

COLTON HATED TO leave her alone like that, but she, at least, had been conscious, eating and moving well—up until now. But it seemed to hit her like a ton of bricks while she ate. He made his way to his room and sat down. He hadn't been here long when a soldier knocked on his door, saying he had an important phone call. Following the man, Colton hoped it was Mason responding to the message he'd left for him earlier.

"What the hell happened?" Mason asked.

It was with a relief of sorts that Colton told him the whole story.

"Holy shit," Mason said. "Are you guys okay?"

"I am. Kate'll be all right, but I don't know about George. I haven't had an update."

"I'll find out," Mason said. "And Kate'll make it?"

"She's shaky, but she was up, moving around, and she ate well at dinnertime but then crashed. She's in bed now."

"That hypothermia is deadly," Mason said, with a note of warning.

"I know. I don't really want to leave her alone, but she didn't want company."

"Is this Kate? As in *Kate*, Kate?"

Colton winced at that, having forgotten Mason had seen him the morning after he'd been with her. "Yeah," he said heavily. "It's her."

At that, Mason whistled. "Wow. Looks like we've done it again."

"Hell, no," Colton said indignantly. "That's your shit, not mine."

"Apparently it affects everybody who is part of my group," Mason said, chuckling. "And make sure you work things out while you're alive and well because, if somebody tried once to kill her, you don't know that they won't try again."

"We have to figure out whether she was the target or George," Colton said.

"Yes, but, from a safety perspective at this point, it doesn't matter which one it was," Mason said. "Because, even if it was George, chances are they'll be afraid she saw something. So watch it, or you'll end up losing her before you ever get her back again. That means, you could be at risk as well. Now are you sure you're feeling okay?"

By the time the phone call ended, Colton was a little more disturbed than he'd wanted to consider. Just because he was here for a training mission didn't mean other people wouldn't be around who couldn't be trusted. It was a small group, and they were doing Arctic training. He didn't even know for sure who was coming in. He wasn't supposed to be here himself originally, but a lecturer had stepped aside on short notice, and the leader had asked for assistance. So, of course, Colton had stepped up.

Besides, Troy had asked for help. Now, if Colton could find the guy who sabotaged the cargo plane, then maybe things could move forward at a regular pace. The courses in the training session weren't supposed to start for another three days, and Colton wasn't sure if the inspectors would have enough time to get to the bottom of what had happened to Kate and George by then. Colton was still hoping for a good update on George too. Thinking about Troy, Colton called Mason back. "Hey, one more thing. Any update on Troy?"

"He's arriving tomorrow," came back the answer. He was already in transit, which would explain why Colton hadn't heard anything.

"So, is there any way you can get me a laptop and a phone?"

"I know one of the guys who's coming for your training. He should have landed already. Let me see if I can get something from the base for you. It would only be basic-level equipment but—"

"I lost everything," Colton said. "I'll have to talk to the insurance adjuster about it, I guess, but there won't likely be anything worth claiming."

"Cell phone, laptop, what else?"

"Personals, gear, toiletries, that's it."

"Let me talk to the base and see what we can do."

And, with that, Colton had to be satisfied. They ended the call, and he returned to the barracks, grabbed the towel he'd been given and walked to the showers, where he stood under the hot water and scrubbed. When he finally dried off, he put on his same clothes again and headed back to his room. He didn't see another soul while he was there. This was normally a fairly isolated place, and he preferred that in most instances. But tonight he would have liked to have a bit of access to the outside world.

In the middle of the night, he woke up but didn't understand why. He lay here, listening for sounds, but he didn't hear anything out of the ordinary. A wind had picked up outside and was definitely howling as it vented around the buildings, trying to bend them to its will. But instead it just left a weird eerie feeling.

Not exactly sure what was going on, he hopped out of bed, threw on his pants, and, barefoot, padded down toward Kate's room. He listened outside her door and heard her whimpering inside. He knocked gently, and, when he got no answer, he opened the door and stepped inside. The room was in darkness, but he didn't need a light to see her pale skin as she tossed on the bed, the sheet barely covering any of her. He grabbed the sheet and blankets and pulled them around her. He sat down beside her, his hand going to her cheek as he gently stroked it and whispered, "You're safe now, Kate. It's okay."

She whimpered again, curling against his hand, while he gently used his other to stroke the side of her face and her hair. "I'm so sorry this happened to you," he said. "It will get better."

CHAPTER 5

K ATE WOKE UP with a start, caught between the arctic chill of her nightmare and the heated warmth of somebody's hand. Somebody she recognized, bringing back a longing from years before. She stared up at Colton's familiar face and gasped. "Oh, my God. How long will the nightmares last?"

"Quite a while probably," he said, and, picking up her hand, he held it against his cheek. "It will get better though. I can promise you that."

She shook her head. "It just seemed like all I could think about was the engine blowing up and the wing falling off and the crash," she said. "The parachuting down wasn't a problem, but, when I slammed into that icy-cold water, everything inside me went numb. I don't know how I stayed afloat as long as I did."

"I'm grateful you did," Colton said, "because it was hard enough to keep George afloat. Once you started to sink too, I knew I couldn't hold both of you up for long."

"I don't know how you did it at all. But I knew George needed to stay up," she said. "He has a family. Those boys need their father."

"That doesn't make your life any less valuable." Colton stroked the sweaty strands of hair off her face. "Can you sleep again now?"

She rolled over, blowing out a long sigh, and stared at the small room. "I guess," she said. She could hear the wind howling around the small building. "It's such a strange location, isn't it?"

"I like it. I didn't realize the actual training I came for wasn't due to start for another couple days though."

"Are you giving or receiving?"

"I wasn't supposed to be here at all, but Troy is doing some of the instruction, and he needed a hand, so I'll be helping him teach as well."

Kate laughed at that. "Me, I'm just spare baggage apparently," and then she started to shiver again. She cried out, "Oh, my God, I'm so damn cold all the time."

Colton grabbed another blanket and piled it on top of her. She curled up underneath, but no way he couldn't feel her shivering underneath. "I need more clothes," she said, struggling to keep her teeth from chattering.

"Do you want me to grab your T-shirt?"

"I already put it back on at some point," she said. "It's amazing how much not having pajamas makes a difference."

"You're used to California. Out there it's not necessary to wear anything to bed."

"No," she said. "Except when I get chilled, when I get *really* chilled." She lay underneath the blankets, shuddering in the darkness. "What time is it anyway?"

"I think it's just around midnight, but maybe it's a little after."

"And, of course, we have no cell phones," she said, then groaned. "I think I still had a year to pay on that contract too. Damn it."

He smiled. "I'm sure there'll be some compensation for this, wouldn't you think?"

"At least I didn't have my laptop," she said. "I stopped packing it when the phones got so advanced. What about you?"

"My laptop, other electronics, my phone, my personal gear," he said cheerfully. "Yep. All gone."

"How can you be so chipper about it?" she muttered, focused on the upcoming hassle of dealing with the phone contract and getting a new phone. "I wonder if we can even get phones up here."

"If we go into town, we can," he said, "but you might want to wait until you get back to the States."

"Yeah," she said, stifling a yawn. "*If* I'm going home in another day anyway, it'll be inconvenient, but I'll survive."

"It really goes to show how much our world has changed," Colton said. "That we can't go anywhere without feeling lost without technology."

"It's a convenience. An instant gratification. I can get my emails. I get chat messages from family and friends. And I can check the weather," she said, with a hand wave to the window. "From the gusty winds out there, it sounds like a hell of a storm."

"I don't think it's a storm at all," he said. "I think it's literally just wind."

"You're kidding? That's depressing," she said, and again another yawn took over.

"But back to our phones. I like always being able to check the time," Colton said with a smile. He straightened, and Kate watched sadly as he walked to the doorway.

"Why did you never call me?" she asked impulsively.

He stopped, looked at her in surprise and turned the tables on her. "Why did you never call me?"

"It felt weird to," she said honestly. "I kept hoping you'd

call me."

His smile flashed in delight. "And maybe I was hoping you'd call me too," he teased.

"I guess I'm not as modern and forward-thinking as I thought," she said. "Because it didn't feel right, you know? I knew you were really busy, and so was I."

"So why don't we leave it as, *It just wasn't the right time.*" He gave her a gentle smile and said, "Now I'll head back to bed. Try to get some sleep." He shut the door softly behind him.

She lay here, listening to the wind howling outside, thinking about his words about it not being the right time.

So when was the right time? Was there a right time? Or had that right time come and gone, and she had failed to pick up the opportunity when it came by? She had wanted to spend a lot more time with him but felt awkward about trying to call him the morning after—as if they had this odd system in place, where it was for one night only and never again.

At the time she hadn't been looking for anything more, but she couldn't stop thinking about him afterward, and it had bothered her that she never got the chance to see him again, that she never heard back from him. He'd been busy off on missions; she'd been busy flying all over the place. And yet, in all those years, they still hadn't reconnected. And now, of all the times for them to connect, she had to admit this was one of the best times for it. After all, he had saved George's life.

He had saved her life too.

As questions ran through her mind, she lay tucked under the blankets, trying desperately to warm up again. She understood it would take time, and sometimes she thought she was doing better, and then, all of a sudden, she wouldn't be so good. This was one of those times. She realized, now that she was wide awake, how she needed to get up and go to the bathroom. And that meant putting more clothes on to get down the hallway. Only to take away some once there.

She grabbed her pants and pulled them on, then slipped the still-damp socks over her bare feet. She opened the door and moved as quickly and as quietly as she could to the communal bathroom. Once inside, she used the facilities, washed up and opened the door to step back out. She almost screamed at the tall figure standing in front of her.

"Easy," Colton said.

"Oh, my gosh," she said, "you scared me."

"Sorry. I didn't mean to, but I heard you running this way and wanted to make sure you were okay."

"So, the problem with being cold and awake," she said, "is that my bladder won't stop calling to me."

"It's to be expected. You'd have the same problem any-time you woke up, but the cold just makes it harder to ignore."

"True enough." Stepping out, she said, "It's empty now, if you need to use it."

"I'll just follow you back to your room."

She looked up at him in surprise. "Any reason for that?"

"The escort? Just being a gentleman," he said smoothly.

She snorted. "Well, the last time we met, and you were escorting me to the bedroom, a gentleman you were not."

"Hey," he said. "Now that was a two-way street."

"It was, indeed. I guess I wasn't much of a lady, at that," she said with a laugh. In truth, the sex had been hot and heavy and hadn't stopped from the time they'd started to the time they had to leave. "It took me days to recover from that night," she said with a laugh.

"Me too," Colton said. "We were a couple rabbits."

"That sounds terrible," she protested.

He burst out laughing. "It didn't sound very classy, did it?"

"Nope," she said. "It sounds disgusting, but it's very honest." At her door she smiled up at him. "Thanks for the escort." She frowned and mumbled, "Wait. I didn't leave a light on."

"What was that?" He turned to face her, a questioning look on his face.

"I didn't turn my light on before I left," she said, "but look. The lamp is on." Colton stepped inside, closed the door behind her and held a finger up to his lips. She nodded, but nobody could have hidden in this tiny space she called her room. There was a closet, but it had no door, and it was open and empty, as far as she could see. There was the bed, and the only option was under it.

Colton dropped to the floor and checked, but it was empty.

"What the devil?" Kate said, turning to look around. "Am I losing my mind?"

"I don't think so. Maybe it wasn't you who I heard running."

She stared at him. "To the bathroom? I wasn't running. I moved fast—as fast as I could, given the circumstances—because I was cold, but I didn't run."

"No," he said. "Now that I think about it, I should have known. Damn it." He ran his hand through his hair, frustrated. "Somebody else was running down the hallway. You wouldn't have been in the bathroom long enough by the time I was standing there." He frowned, then turned and said, "The chances of catching anybody at this point are nonexistent. They are long gone."

"But why would somebody have been in my room anyway?" Kate asked softly. Confusion and fear spiked through her. "How would anybody have known where I was?"

"We are new arrivals," Colton said, "and got here with a fair bit of excitement, I'm sure. So it's not hard to imagine other people know we're here. Remember how it was when we were at dinner in the mess hall?"

"I get that." Kate looked around and sighed. "It doesn't make me feel any better though."

"My room has bunks," he said, "so you're welcome to grab one, if you want."

She thought about it and then nodded. "You know what? Maybe I should. I don't think I'd sleep another wink knowing somebody was in here. Particularly as I don't know why."

Colton looked around and said, "Do you have anything in here to move?"

She shook her head. "I'm wearing it, except my boots."

"Good. Maybe that also confused him, except that the blankets were turned back, so it's obvious somebody had been sleeping there. Come on. Let's go."

He left the light on, then shut the door. He also set a hair in such a way that, if somebody opened the door, it would fall. She watched him but didn't question it. He just smiled and led her to his room. There, he said, "I'm in the bottom bunk. Are you okay with the top?"

She nodded, shivering still, and said, "At this point"— her teeth chattering again—"I just want to get warm."

"Up you go," he said, "and maybe I'll return to your room and grab those blankets."

"Unless you have some here," she said. He checked the closet and pulled out two. He tossed them over her and tucked her in as much as he could from where he stood. She rolled over against the wall and muttered, "Good night." She waited until he settled back into his own bunk before she relaxed.

A part of her wondered about taking their relationship back to the same level it had been. Only she didn't want to go backward because she didn't want what they'd had, since that had been based solely on sex. She wanted to go forward to something better; she just didn't know how to get there. She wasn't very good at relationships. She'd had plenty of them, but they never lasted more than a few months.

She thought she was a giving, caring person and didn't understand why her relationships kept breaking down. One man had said she didn't seem to care enough, and another had said she cared too much. She figured she couldn't win. Her mother always told her that she just hadn't met the right man and that he'd come along eventually. She didn't know about that either because she'd dated a lot, and there certainly wasn't any sign of the right man for her coming around.

Her mom also hadn't really liked any of the men she'd brought home either. And Kate never introduced someone to her parents unless she had been seeing them for several months. She had tried living with one guy, thinking it was a step in the right direction, but she couldn't handle it. He had been such a messy person to live with, expecting her to be his maid, that she'd found herself screaming at him. He had finally packed up and walked out on her.

She knew she'd overreacted, but, when his hair was everywhere from his shaving—all over the mirror, the sink and the faucets, and he hadn't cleaned up any of it, clearly expecting her to—she'd come undone. She had already had the pick-up-after-yourself conversation with him. Yet his socks and clothes remained on the floor. Until he left. For once he had picked up after himself.

After that, she muted her responses a lot and often checked out the guy's bathroom to see how bad it was. She figured, just out of respect and common courtesy for others, plus a sense of self-responsibility, that people would clean up their own messes, but apparently that wasn't a theory held by all. It was such a dumb thing to have lost it over, but it had been an accumulation of his other aspects. He had just looked at her, like she was being so picky. He had said, if she didn't like it, why wasn't she cleaning it up?

On that note, she stopped wondering about the vagaries of relationships and the problems within them. Then she closed her eyes and let sleep snag her up and take her under again.

COLTON WOKE UP the next morning and froze. Something was different. Then he realized the breathing he heard was Kate above him. He slid out of bed and checked on her. She slept heavily. He picked up his blanket and tossed it over her, so she'd have yet another layer of warmth and headed to the bathroom. He used the facilities, scrubbed his teeth, and washed his face and hair. Realizing it had to be at least sevenish from the light outside, he headed to her assigned room.

At the door, he squatted to see the hair was still in place, so nobody had entered the room since. He stepped back into his room and finished dressing, then made up his bunk without the blanket and slipped out again. If he could find coffee, he'd bring a cup back for her. As he headed toward the mess tent, the base commander stepped out of a building and called him over.

Colton saluted and was told, "At ease, son. Come in and take a seat." As Colton sat down, the commander said, "You want to tell me what happened yesterday?"

He raised his eyebrows. "Yesterday?"

The commander waved his hand. "You guys crashed in the ocean and were picked up, correct?"

Colton nodded.

"Can you give me any details on the flight?"

Colton gave him a rundown, adding, "We lost everything, from our cell phones, my laptop and our personal gear and bags."

"Good thing you weren't taking off on a big holiday," the commander said with a half smirk. "You could have lost a lot more."

"So true. We do need to roust up some cell phones though, as soon as possible."

"I hear you. I have a laptop you can probably use. I was talking to a couple men at the Coronado base."

Colton frowned. "Was it Mason?"

"Yes, Mason. Smart man. He's asked for you to have a laptop for your use while you're here, and he's airlifting a cell phone for you."

"Good," Colton said. "That would be helpful. And the laptop would be appreciated."

"Mind telling me what it is you plan on doing with it?"

Colton lowered his voice and said, "Looking into the sabotage issue, sir."

The commander nodded. "We do have MPs too, you

know? Now, son, I can't have you going around half-cocked, thinking you're James Bond."

"More like Sherlock, sir," Colton said with a smile.

"Same diff as far as I'm concerned. You can work with my MPs, who will be assigned to this investigation. How long are you supposed to be here?"

"I was tagged to help Troy on an upcoming training session."

"That may have to get pushed back a few days," the commander said. "We've got a really ugly weather front coming in, and, when I say *ugly*, I mean ugly. Nobody is going outside if it remains like that."

"Wow," Colton said. "I hadn't expected that."

"Nope, I don't imagine you did. We've got a bunch of guys coming in early for the training too. But nobody will be training outside if that weather doesn't lighten up. We'll put them up for a few days, but, if need be, we'll cancel the whole thing."

Colton nodded. "I guess the supplies don't last long if you're multiplying your numbers and keeping the men inside."

"We're well supplied, and I don't give a rat's ass about the cost, but keeping you all out of trouble when you're bored stiff is not my cup of tea," he said. "I expect good behavior from everybody visiting my base."

"Absolutely, sir."

The commander stood and asked, "And what about her? What kind of trouble will she be?"

Colton jumped to his feet. "None, I believe, sir."

"She already is," the commander said with a grimace. "She's young. She's attractive, and she's a pilot. My boys have already noticed. Believe me."

"Speaking of which," Colton said and then frowned, wondering if he should mention it.

The commander dropped back into his seat and said, "Speak up, son."

"She had a visitor last night. And it wasn't an invited visitor." When he explained what happened, the commander's brows drew together, thick and angry. "I sure hope you're not accusing anybody of anything," he said, his gaze slowly searching Colton's.

"Not accusing anybody of anything, sir," Colton said. "Only that somebody went into her room during the middle of the night and then took off running."

"Interesting," the commander said, staring around the room, his fingers thrumming on the table. "We're a small base here. I run a tight ship and don't tolerate anybody causing trouble."

Colton knew the commander was referring to him. He nodded slowly. "Just thought I'd mention it, sir."

"The only reason I'm even paying attention," he said, "is because Mason spoke so highly of you."

"Thank you, sir," Colton said, realizing he would have to build trust with this man, and fast.

"If you hear of anything else happening, you let me know," he said, "but don't go talking to anybody."

"Anybody?"

"No investigative work without my MPs involved."

"Agreed," Colton said. It was standard practice anywhere. The MPs had to be involved.

The commander gave him a hard look. But Colton stared back easily, comfortable with authority. You didn't get anywhere in life if you didn't get along with it somewhat. They had to know they could count on you. And, if there was one thing Colton prided himself on, it was being counted on.

The commander cleared his throat and asked, "Where is she?"

"Still sleeping," Colton admitted. "She didn't have a good night."

"After a trauma like you three survived, I highly doubt anybody would. She probably needs to visit with our resident shrink."

"I'll tell her that when she wakes up."

The commander snorted. "No. Have her come to me when she's awake and had some breakfast. I'd like to see her condition for myself, and it won't be optional. Make that an order."

Colton understood. It was up to the base commander to keep the base and everyone on it safe. If she was traumatized, she would need help, and the sooner she received it, the better, for everyone's sake.

He walked back to the mess hall. Breakfast was available, but he was more interested in coffee. He grabbed a cup for himself and walked over to the window and sat down. The day was still gray with lots of wind. He could see how the weather was heading for an ugly squall but didn't know how long that would last. When somebody sat down at his table, he was surprised to be addressed personally.

"About time you got here, Colton," a familiar voice said.

He turned, his eyes wide as he smiled and reached across, and the two men gripped forearms. "Damn, it's good to see you, Troy," he said. "I thought you weren't in this early."

"That's my line," Troy said with a chuckle. "When you come in for a hard landing, you come in for a hard landing."

"Didn't plan on the hard landing until that plane cracked apart, and we ended up in the Arctic Ocean," Colton said.

"Yeah, so how are you doing?"

"I'm okay, just haven't had much sleep. The copilot's still sleeping, but she had nightmares throughout the night, and I just couldn't sleep."

"It's pretty traumatizing," Troy said. "Any idea what happened?"

"I think we're leaning toward sabotage," Colton said, "but it'll be hard to do much about it from up here."

"Not necessarily," Troy said. "I understand you told Mason?"

"What you mean is, you've already talked to Mason," Colton said with a chuckle.

"Well, I might have," Troy said. "I came in early to ensure we had all the gear for the training. And then I asked if you could give me a hand with it. But apparently, according to the commander, as of this morning, it's looking like the training may be pushed off a couple days, due to ugly weather."

"I don't know if that's good or bad," Colton said. "The longer I'm here, the more I'll just think."

"You'll do what you can do from here. I'm sure the Coronado base is doing a full search, as is the Halifax base and the international airport."

"I didn't see anybody around the plane," he said.

"Doesn't mean it wasn't put on in Coronado," Troy said. "You also have to consider a remote detonation."

Colton stared at him. "That's a long way for a remote detonation."

"Not if it was somebody else's cell phone," he said.

"What if that phone—say your copilot's—rang while you were up there? And maybe she answered it, and it triggered an alarm to blow up the plane?"

Colton froze. "You know what? I was sitting there, half dozing, and I did hear a phone. I don't know how close to the engine blowing up that was though."

"Everybody else is thinking a timer had to be on it maybe," Troy said. "But I would think it's much more likely that somebody called her number, or George's, and, as soon as that phone rang, it triggered the bomb itself."

"God, I should have thought of that already," Colton said, shaking his head. "It's just been so crazy that it hadn't even crossed my mind."

"That's why I'm here to help," Troy said, smiling broadly. "You know how much I love a good mystery."

"Good thing," Colton said, "because this one is looking a little too convoluted, or we're just making it that way when it's damn obvious."

"I understand George is up as a witness against some of his coworkers."

"Yes, we spoke of it a little, while I was keeping some fight in him in that icy water," Colton said. "Damn, I should have asked the commander for an update on him. He might have an answer faster than Mason."

"We'll see the commander later," Troy said. "We can always ask him then."

Colton nodded. "I hear you. I was planning on taking coffee back to Kate, but the longer she sleeps, the better."

"*Kate*, is it?"

"Yep," Colton confirmed without saying anything. But he knew from the twinkle in Troy's eye that Troy already knew. "Mason?"

Troy gave a casual shrug as he settled back, a smile playing at the corner of his lips. "Maybe," he said. "But it wasn't just the two of you at that big party that night all those years ago."

"Shit," Colton said. "Were you there too?"

"I was. I had my eye on her too, but she only saw you."

"Well, considering that she's tucked up in the top bunk above my bed right now, that night didn't make too much of an impression."

Colton kept to himself their discussion about why he'd never called because he didn't have a good answer, except that some things you just knew were a minefield. As much as he'd wanted to stay and to be with her, it would have changed his life completely, and he just hadn't been ready. He meant it when he had said it wasn't the right time. That didn't necessarily mean it wasn't the right time for her, but it wasn't the right time for him to have a relationship. He wondered if now was the better time.

Yet, when he looked back on it and thought about decisions he had made, sometimes he had to wonder where his head was that he would walk away from someone so gorgeous, kind and caring like her.

"She's a really nice girl," Troy said. "And, if the time is right for you guys now, that's perfect."

"Whoa, whoa, whoa," Colton said. "It's hardly anything that serious."

"You've been through a hell of a bonding experience," Troy said, chuckling. "So, breakfast first or do you want to go wake her?"

"She needs sleep." Colton looked at the food, raised his nose tentatively and said, "Besides, the food is fresh and hot right now." He looked at Troy. "You?"

"Absolutely. Come on. Let's go." And, with that, the two men walked toward the food line.

CHAPTER 6

KATE WOKE UP in a haze of warmth, immediately aware of the aroma of coffee. Her eyes flew open to see a smiling Colton in front of her, holding a big mug of hot coffee.

"That better be for me," she croaked. She cleared her throat and tried again with a smile this time. "And thank you."

He chuckled. "I don't know if you have a place up there to put this," he said, studying the area and then shaking his head. "Better to have you get up and get dressed, or maybe sit up so you can hold it at least."

"The only clothes I've got, I'm already wearing," she said, but she shifted to lean crosswise against the wall and crossed her legs, pulling her blankets up. Then she reached out a hand for the mug. Colton stood on his bunk so he could hand it to her. As soon as the transfer was made, she sagged back and held it, eyes closed. "Nothing quite like hot coffee first thing in the morning," she murmured, her eyes still closed as she let the warmth of the cup bathe her face.

"An interesting reaction," he said. "First you were almost aggressive, and then, when you realized you were getting coffee," he said, "you're just like a sleepy kitten."

"Unless you try to take it away from me," she said and then laughed. "I do appreciate it, by the way." She looked at him. "Have you eaten already too?"

He nodded. "At least an hour ago."

She wrinkled her nose. "Did I miss breakfast?"

"I don't think you missed it," he said. "I think food should be available for at least another half hour."

"Well, I better get up and moving so I get there in time."

Colton thought about it for a moment and then said, "Maybe I can bring you a plate, if you want."

"If you could, that would be really lovely."

"Let me go see," he said. "Every base has different rules."

Kate nodded. "If you can't, let me know, so I have enough time to get there, okay? But I really am still tired and so damn cold."

"Stay there, and I'll check it out." He disappeared from in front of her, slipping quietly out the door. She waited, aware of the passage of time. She was still sleepy, but getting that warm coffee down was her priority. The fact that she even got to wake up today was something she was incredibly blessed to do, and she could only hope George had woken up too. She didn't want to think about losing him. He was a good pilot and a good man.

He had done what was right, and, although some people wouldn't agree with his choice, he was trying to do the right thing. Because military personnel using military flights for something like drug running wasn't anyone they could ever count on. Those were the selfish users of the world, and every company—whether government, military, or large corporations—knew that was a cancer which had to be removed.

Just when she was nearing the bottom of her cup, the door opened, and Colton entered with a large tray. She stared at the food in delight. "Wow, it must have been okay then. Thanks!" She tossed back the last of her coffee and shifted into a better position. From that viewpoint, she realized Colton hadn't come alone. "Hi, I'm Kate," she said. "Who are you?"

"Troy Landry." He reached out a hand and said, "I'd shake, but you're a little far away."

"Consider it shaken," she said, as she leaned forward to grab the tray from Colton. "This looks absolutely wonderful." She stared down at the food. "So did you pick up all this for the three of us, or have you both eaten?"

"We've both eaten," Troy said, laughing. "So, if you think you can do justice to that, then go for it."

Kate beamed at him. "I can do fair justice to it, and I'm so cold that I figure an extra bit of food wouldn't hurt."

"You need it," Colton said. "So dig in."

She nodded. "Will the coffee shut down too?"

Colton reached up a hand for her cup, and it took a little bit of maneuvering to not spill the tray, but she got the empty cup to him, and the two men disappeared again. She tucked right into the food, starting with sausages, bacon, eggs and toast. Pancakes were underneath as well. By the time the guys returned with a cup of coffee, they were joking back and forth, and her plate was half gone.

Colton looked at it and said, "I'm glad to see you've got an appetite."

"More than I expected," she mumbled, chewing a bite of toast. She stared at the coffee with longing. "If you can just find a place to put that for the moment, I'll get to it soon." He nodded, put it down and then held up two big cookies. Her eyes widened. "I can't eat those."

"I was thinking of later," he said.

She smiled. "That sounds good. At least they won't

starve us up here."

"No," Colton said, "but the base commander does want to speak with you."

Her stomach clenched tight at that, but she nodded. "To be expected. I do need to offer my appreciation for the assistance and care I've been shown."

"That would be the prudent thing. By the way, he's also a little touchy about any talk of sabotage."

"But it wouldn't have been done here," she said, studying the two men.

"That brings up a question," Colton said. "Just before the explosion, did either of you receive a phone call?"

Kate frowned, then thought back and nodded. "I'm not exactly sure of the timing, but I did get a call. Why?"

"Did you look at the Caller ID or answer the call?"

"Nobody was there. I think it was a private caller, but no one answered when I clicked on it."

Troy looked at Colton and nodded.

"What does that mean?" she asked suspiciously.

"It means, the bomb could have been installed earlier," Colton said, "but we think it was triggered by the phone call to you."

She frowned. "What? Meaning, if I hadn't answered, it wouldn't have blown up?"

"No. It probably would have blown up regardless, maybe after a certain number of rings or even when voicemail kicked in, but the fact that you did pick it up meant it triggered the detonation when it did."

Her mind churned on the possibilities. She swallowed hard. "Well, that sucks."

"When people want to do something like this," Troy said, "they do it and don't leave much to chance."

She nodded.

"There wasn't much left to chance on this," Colton said. "And there's not much left out there to find."

"Will they do any recovery?" she asked.

"I doubt it because it was a small plane, and there won't be much left," Colton said, "but we can't be sure about that. Still, it's out of our hands."

"It's not like my cell phone is of any value now," Kate said.

"I don't even think that's the issue as much as the fact that it's debris they don't want to leave everywhere."

"That makes sense too," she said. "It's still sad though to hear it was a preset bomb."

"It is," Colton said. "But it could be much worse if, say, George's body was out there too. Then they might consider a recovery operation."

"Right," she said.

"I would guess the commander also wants to get your first-hand impression of what happened."

"Including the phone call?" she asked cautiously.

Troy frowned. And then he gave a clipped nod. "I would tell him. He's not stupid. And, if it was sabotage, he'll suspect a remote detonator as well."

"How many people would have your number?" Colton asked.

Kate winced. "Dozens, if not hundreds," she admitted. "I've had this number for a really long time."

"It could get difficult then," Colton said, "because I'm sure an investigation will involve everybody on your contact list."

"Why?" she asked in confusion. "It said Unknown Number or Private Number of the like."

"Which means it was probably a burner phone, but how many people could possibly know your number and not be on your contact list?"

"I don't know," she said. "Anybody I work with and anybody my friends may have passed my number on to, although I'm fairly strict about that," she admitted.

"That's good to know," Troy said. "The thing is, somebody had it, and somebody may have used it to blow up the plane."

"What about George's phone?" she asked, desperately trying to deflect interest from her phone. "There was no need for someone after George to use my phone."

"What about your ex-boyfriend?" Colton asked. "George mentioned he'd made threats."

"Yes," she said, getting angry, her tone sharp and to the point. "I was lonely and hooked up when I shouldn't have. When I tried to break it off, he became very possessive. Very stalkerish," she added. And then she shook her head. "I'm not mad at you guys. I'm just mad at the situation with my ex. The relationship developed so quickly that I didn't have any warning he was some sort of psycho."

"Would he have had anything to do with something like this?"

"I have no idea," she said. "I think George was afraid he might have, but it doesn't make any sense to me."

"Nothing does on a deal like this," Troy said. "These scenarios are just plain ugly, and there is no real way to know who and what might be involved yet."

"No, but you're already targeting my phone," she said, "and, because my phone is on the bottom of the Arctic Ocean, we'll never know all the contacts on it."

"Did you ever transfer or download your contact list?"

"No," she said slowly, "but my old phone is at home."

"Good," Troy said. "That's a place to start."

"I really don't like the way you're thinking," she mumbled, and she picked up another chunk of sausage and chewed on it as she glared at him. "My friends wouldn't do this."

"Of course not," he said in surprise. "No true *friend* would. The thing is, lots of people on your contact list are probably more like acquaintances or work associates, not friends. And you don't know if someone else's phone was compromised to get your number."

She preferred that thought.

"We also need to know more about your boyfriend," Colton said.

Something was off in his tone. She shot him a glance. "That's *ex*-boyfriend, please," she said, "and, for the record, if I'd had any understanding of just what a psycho he was, I'd have never gone out with him."

"How long were you with him?"

"That's just it. I wasn't 'with him'—not in the way you think. We dated, maybe five or six times over the course of two weeks," she admitted. "Everything was fine until we were at a restaurant one night, and my dinner was a little cold. He got all angry and uppity about it and wanted both of our meals for free because of it and raised a hell of a scene. I was really embarrassed and told him that wasn't the kind of behavior I was interested in being around. He ended up turning on me, saying he was just the kind of person who did what everybody else wanted to do but didn't have the balls for and that I should never criticize him, especially not in front of anyone."

Colton stared at her in surprise.

"The whole thing was really shocking, and he said a lot more, but you can get the gist. When I got home that night, I was pretty shaken over the whole thing and sent him a text saying I didn't want to see him again." She held up a hand. "I know. I know. Not cool. I should have done it in person."

"Maybe not in this case," Colton said. "Doing it in person would likely have triggered him to be violent."

"I have to admit that's exactly what I was thinking and why I did it that way," she said. "The trouble is, by the time I figured out how dangerous he was, he was already well and truly pissed at me."

"Did he respond to the text?"

"Yeah," she said with a wry smile. "He sure did. It was like, 'No one breaks up with me, bitch' or something very close to that." She watched the looks crossing the faces of both men. "Right? Talk about warning signs. Just a little too late," she said sadly.

"How bad did it get after that?"

"Pretty ugly. He kept calling and texting me, and then he left notes at my apartment building and then signs on my door. He slipped nasty threatening letters under my door, and he came to my work once. Of course I travel a lot anyway, and—"

"What does he do?" Colton asked.

"He's another navy pilot," she said, slowly meeting his gaze. "It's one of the reasons I thought maybe it would work out. Someone who would understand my work and my travel schedule. We had some things in common, and honestly, well, I was lonely."

Colton nodded but didn't say anything.

She could still feel something coming off him. It wasn't judgment exactly, but it was almost as if he was unhappy about it. But it wasn't like he'd been around to keep her company, so whatever. She just shrugged and kept eating. "I was taking every job I could just to stay away from him. Then this flight came up, and I was like, perfect, but as you can see, *perfect* didn't work out so well."

"I don't think perfect worked out at all," Colton said quietly. "Sounds like it was a pretty raw deal."

"Feels like it too," she said. She put the tray down beside her, even though she hadn't finished.

Troy looked at it and said, "If you can eat more, you should."

She shrugged, but her mind and heart weren't on the food anymore.

"Do you think he would have attacked you at home?" Colton asked.

"Yes," she said, "I was at the point of talking to the MPs about him."

"So did you?"

"I made the appointment, but this flight came up, so I had to cancel it." She stared at Colton moodily. "And now I'm left to wonder what would have happened if I had stayed and kept that appointment."

"Probably nothing different," he said. "If he was behind this, something else would have triggered it."

"Or not," she said. "Because, in a rash move, I told him that I'd made an appointment and would make a complaint."

Both men stared at her.

She shrugged. "Like I said, I haven't done anything right in this whole deal since it started. All I can tell you is that I needed to do something to send him away, and I had hoped the threat of reporting him would do it."

"Well, it did something," Colton said harshly, "but I don't think it was what you were hoping for."

Troy and Colton shared a long look, silently communicating.

"I know," Kate said. "You both think I should file a complaint as soon as we're back at Coronado." She sighed heavily. "So do I."

"Good," Colton said, a note of finality in his tone. "I'll be notifying Mason of your stalker and his threats when I report in next. Your witness statement is critical supporting evidence."

COLTON COULDN'T UNDERSTAND the jealousy boiling inside him. He understood the need to have companionship because someone was lonely. Hell, he'd done the same thing himself. It just bothered him that she'd been so lonely to turn to some lousy guy like that. But, then again, as she said, he'd seemed perfect on the surface, and then the shadows had shown up.

And, once the decline had happened, it happened fast. Colton got the guy's name, Ned Bertram, and wrote it down. "We'll have to get some of this onto the MPs desk," he said. He looked at Kate's tray and said, "Troy's right. If you can eat a little more, you should. Then let's get you to the base commander and afterward to the MPs."

She nodded. "Presumably all of them will connect from base to base?"

"I doubt it," Troy said cheerfully. "That sounds like way too much communication for them. But we can make sure it gets to the bases we need to contact."

She smiled and snagged up the last half of her toast and

then handed over the tray, munching on her toast while she clambered down the ladder. "I need to make a pit stop first," she said, then looked at her boots and managed to get into them without too much difficulty and headed to the bathroom. When she was done, the guys were standing outside the door, waiting for her.

"Are you guys like my security detail?" she asked. "Because that won't be fun."

"Let's call it a friendly escort instead," Colton said.

She laughed and tucked her arm into the crook of his elbow, and he pulled her close against it. As they walked down the hallways, he told her about the training being delayed because of the weather.

She frowned. "But wouldn't that make for a better training session?"

Troy laughed. "*Oooh!* She'd like to see you suffer, wouldn't she?"

"Not really," Kate said. "I just wondered because, if it's supposed to be for arctic conditions, wouldn't rough outdoor conditions be perfect?"

"The base commander gets to make that decision," Colton said. "What they can't have are fatalities."

An officer approached them up ahead. Smiling, he introduced himself as Petty Officer John Parsons. "How are you doing?" he asked Kate.

"I'm doing fine. Thank you, sir," Kate said with a smile.

"The base commander would like to see you."

She nodded. "I would be happy to see him as well."

Parsons led the way through the building out to several offshoot buildings. Finally they ended up at a large office. The officer knocked on the door, and they were invited to enter. They stepped inside, saluting as required. The commander looked up, and, seeing who it was, stood and walked around the desk to greet Kate.

"Glad to see you looking so well. Please, everyone, have a seat. When I heard the first reports, I wasn't sure what we had."

"I wasn't so sure myself, sir." Kate hesitated and asked, "Have you had any update on how George is doing?"

"He's still holding his own, though a chance still remains that he'll lose fingers and toes."

She winced at that. "I'm sure he won't appreciate that. He's a fine man and an excellent pilot. I would hate to see his career ended prematurely."

"The doctors are working on it. You seem to have come out of it rather well."

"I'm certainly better after getting some sleep," she said, "but I am fully aware I wouldn't be here today if it wasn't for Colton being on board."

The commander looked at Colton and nodded. "Funny, he said something similar about you earlier today."

She laughed. "George and I did what we could to issue a Mayday call and to bring down the plane in an unpopulated area, but Colton was the one handing out parachutes and kicking us out of the plane. Literally. And then, when we were in the air, he obviously navigated himself to ensure he would land as close to both of us as possible.

"He saved George, holding him up nearly the whole time we were in the water and encouraging him to soldier on and to fight to live. I fared better initially, but eventually I was going under too, so he dragged my butt back to the surface and held on to me also," she said with a smile. "But honestly, sir? It's you to whom all three of us owe our lives. Sending the cruiser out to grab us, that was huge. We couldn't hold on much longer."

He gave her a deferential nod, acknowledging her thanks. "Glad you all made it. You'll be here for a few more days, what with the bad weather rolling in," he said, "and it's coming in even faster than expected. I don't think we'll get the flights in that we expected, and I doubt we'll be getting any out either. So get comfortable because you'll be here for a bit."

Her eyebrows raised. "I heard the heavy winds in the night, and I had to wonder how bad the weather would get."

"Bad enough," he said cheerfully. "But, as soon as we can, we'll fly you out."

She smiled and nodded. "I'll accept the rest and the food gratefully, sir. Actually I just finished a big breakfast and coffee."

"Good," he said. "One of the things I do want you to do is write down exactly what you remember, in as much detail as you can." He walked back to his desk, picked up a pad of paper and a pen, and handed both to her. "Return it to me when you're done, please."

She nodded and smiled. Dismissed, they moved back out of the office, and Petty Officer Parsons said, "Let's get you down to the MPs office now."

Once again they fell into step behind him as he led the way back and around. Finally they came to another office. He rapped on the open door and stepped inside, with the three of them following. Only one man was in the office. He stood and motioned at the seats in front of his desk. "So you must be our unexpected guest."

"Yes," Kate said, sounding hesitant. She sat down and said, "The commander just asked me to write down everything I remember from the accident."

He nodded. "That would be a good place to start." Looking at Colton and Troy, he asked, "Which one of you is Colton?"

"That would be me," Colton said. "And, yes, I do believe this was sabotage."

"Your basis for that?"

Colton took a moment to gather his thoughts and then gave the most clear and concise accounting he could. When he added in the phone call just before the engine exploded, the officer shook his head.

"That could be coincidence."

"Yes, it could be," Colton said. "In many ways, it's the perfect crime because it's not like anyone can retrieve the evidence out there."

The MP looked off into the distance and then shook his head. "Not likely. No. If it were a big passenger jet or something, then potentially we could, but, as it is, we don't have any proof of sabotage either."

"And we won't get any," Kate said, "because of the fact that you aren't going after that line of inquiry."

"No," he said. "That's not my call."

She sagged. "So we just wait until somebody tries to kill us again?"

"Who is it you think might have been behind this?"

"It's hard to say." Colton once again stepped in. "George, the pilot, who is still in critical condition, is testifying as a material witness against two men facing court-martial for using military flights to transport illicit drugs."

"Interesting," the MP said, then made a note of it. "I don't know anything about the case."

"No," Colton said. "It's from Coronado."

"*Ah.*" The officer smiled. "That seems like a big-city

problem. It's not really something we have issues with here."

"Potentially," Kate said bluntly. "But you know how it starts, and that's with just two people."

He smiled at her. "I get it. And I also understand you'll be here for a little longer than you expected."

"Yes," she said. "Until the weather clears."

"It's hard to say when that will be. I'll contact Coronado and see what I can do to be of assistance." And, with that, they were dismissed.

When they walked out, the petty officer was long gone. Colton looked at Troy. "Looks like we're on our own."

"Sounds about right," he said cryptically.

Colton could see the confusion on Kate's face. But he just smiled, tucked her arm into his and said, "How about a cup of tea?"

"That sounds like a good idea. I know I had two cups of coffee with breakfast, but it seems like a long time ago."

"It's been a few hours, so it'll be lunch soon."

At that, she raised her head. She smiled and said, "You know what? I am almost hungry again."

Beside her, Troy let out a big guffaw. "Wow," he said. "She eats like you do."

"Not quite," Colton said cheerfully. "Besides, you need energy for writing down that statement of yours."

"How come I have to, and you don't?" she protested.

He gave her a fat smile. "I already told the commander my story."

"And yet you don't have to write it down?"

"Apparently not," he said. "I was just a passenger though. You were the copilot."

She groaned. "Thanks for reminding me. I'll definitely need something to drink then. Maybe food too." When they entered the cafeteria, Colton picked out a table by the window and parked her there.

"I'll get you something to drink," he said. "You get started on your statement. It might take you a few attempts." She nodded and picked up her pen.

Colton and Troy went for drinks and learned lunch would start in twenty minutes. Colton made a pot of tea and grabbed coffee for himself. With Troy grabbing the teapot, the three of them settled in back at the table. "You might as well get as much done as you can," Colton said, "because the lunch crowd will be in here soon enough."

Just then, the same petty officer they'd met earlier walked up to Colton, handed him a laptop and said, "Compliments of the commander for your use while you are here. The form on top is for you to sign it out." Colton signed the form, acknowledging he would be using the laptop, then he sat down and plugged it in, unsure if the battery was charged or not.

Troy looked at him and said, "That's a good idea. You don't have a cell phone either, do you?"

"Nope," he said, "the only communication I've had is on the base phone."

"Did you call Mason?"

"Well, yeah. I left a message, and he called back, and they tracked me down. Not exactly convenient but now I can communicate directly through chat at least." As soon as he checked his email, he brought up the chat window and contacted Mason, who responded almost immediately. Colton gave him an update, including the fact he now had a laptop but no cell phone yet.

Mason responded that it was in the works, though the weather might delay delivery. With a glance at Kate, Colton added that Kate's old phone was in her apartment, and that it had a contact list on it. Wouldn't have the newest contacts but was still viable as a starting point.

Need her permission to get it.

Colton leaned toward Kate and said, "Mason is asking permission to get into your apartment to get your old cell phone."

Her face blanched, but she nodded. "Top dresser drawer in the right hand corner."

"How does he get in?" he asked.

"What?" she asked mockingly. "Won't they pull some of your ninja stunts and just break in?"

"He could," Colton said, "but it would probably be better if he didn't have to."

She groaned and nodded, then told him the manager had a key, but her girlfriend had one as well. She gave him the names of both. "We'll have to contact my girlfriend and let her know what happened though."

"Right," he said. "I'll get Mason to make that call and see if he can convince her that we need to get in." With that information parlayed, Colton passed on a message with an update of their discussions with the base commander and the MPs. **They'll be cooperative but won't necessarily instigate or open an investigation,** Colton typed.

No, that will probably have to come from Coronado, Mason replied.

Troy also suggested it could have been a remote detonator using a phone call onto Kate's phone.

Makes sense, Mason typed.

Next Colton provided the details of Kate's ex-boyfriend, along with a brief overview of the stalking and threats. **So he is suspect number two. Suspect number one is actually**

two persons, the pair court-martialed, who would be based on George's court case.

And that's already being looked into, Mason wrote. **I'll let you know if there are any updates.**

It would be nice if we got a copy of any reports too, Colton typed, **but I know that won't happen.** He looked at Troy, who was watching but had moved and was sitting where he couldn't read the chat window. **Any help would be appreciated,** he added. **We'll be delayed here for a few days due to the weather, and then I'm supposed to stay and do the training, and they'll ship her back home again.**

We need to make sure that whatever flight leaves is safe, Mason replied.

On that note, Colton signed off, closed the laptop and asked Troy, "Did you bring one?"

"Laptop and cell phone," he said cheerfully.

"I miss my cell phone," Kate said suddenly.

"I do too," Colton said, "but the laptop is a good place to start."

"For you," she said, staring at it.

"Do you want to use it?" And he slid it toward her. She moved the pad of paper off to the side and said, "You know what would be easier? If I told my girlfriend that Mason would be calling."

"Have at it," Colton said with a smile. While they watched, she opened up a webpage and her email program and logged in. Then she contacted her girlfriend via email.

"Perfect," he said. "We obviously need to find a way to get some answers, and, at least, this is a start."

"Yeah, that whole 'we' thing is a stretch. The MPs don't seem that interested in helping around here."

"But, like they said, they don't believe it was sabotage."

"Which is kind of hard to understand," she said, "because seriously it's not that big a jump."

"Maybe," Colton said, "but look where we're at now. It's not like anybody is too worried."

Kate groaned and nodded, then returned the laptop and picked up her pen again. "This is starting to sound like, because they don't believe us, it'll take a second attack to get them to consider anything premeditated is really going on."

"Exactly," Colton said, "which is why you need to be safe."

"I'm worried about George," she said.

"George is safe, already under close watch at the hospital, with its own security," he said. "This is about you. We've got to keep you safe."

"But why me over George? I don't get it."

Troy supplied the answer. "It was your phone that rang."

CHAPTER 7

"**I** CAN'T BELIEVE that the only connection to the plane blowing up is my phone," Kate said in a low whisper. "It could just as easily have been George's phone."

"But it wasn't. It was yours."

"But I'm the copilot," she said. "It doesn't make any sense."

"What does being the copilot have to do with it?" Colton asked.

"Obviously nothing," she snapped, raising both hands in frustration. Just then people started to file in for lunch. She groaned. "Oh, crud, now it'll get busy and noisy in here." She turned back to her task, trying to write down what she needed to say but found that Colton was right. She would have to rewrite this a couple times. It was a matter of a brain dump. She knew the tidbits. Just getting them all down on paper and then putting them in logical order which was the challenge.

"I was a last-minute change to the schedule, so it would be interesting to know why the original copilot didn't show up." She tapped the paper, trying to dredge from her mind who was supposed to be there and then shook her head. "We'll have to contact George and ask him."

"I can do that," Troy said, as he pulled out his phone and sent off a text.

"You have contact with the hospital?"

"And I have his commander's number," Troy said. Almost immediately a response came; then he answered back and forth. She waited until finally she couldn't stand it and asked, "Don't you ever share?"

He looked at her in surprise. "Share what?"

"Whatever is going on with your phone right now," she said. "It's obviously got something to do with me."

He gave her a warm smile. "Not really. George is apparently sleeping at the moment, so we won't hear anything back for a while."

She nodded, feeling stupid, went back to her pad of paper and wrote down several more points. Finally she ripped off those two sheets and started again. The men left her alone, which she was grateful for. She looked up a couple times to see the room slowly filling up as everybody came to grab food. Colton and Troy had disappeared. She looked around, shocked, only to see them in the food line. She rolled her eyes when Colton caught sight of her and, grinning, gave her a thumbs-up.

She didn't know if he was planning on picking her up some food and bringing it over so she would keep working or what. Or maybe they would just grab the first round. Her stomach started to growl again, so she'd be happy to have food, but she wanted to get this written statement done first. She quickly finished writing down her notes, crumpled up the extra pages she'd ripped off and tucked them into her pocket, not seeing a trash can nearby. Setting the pad of paper and the pen off to the side, she stood and walked over to join the guys.

"Maybe I'd like to pick out something for myself," she said, peering around their shoulders.

They made room for her in the middle, handed her a tray and a plate, and very quickly she loaded up on hot steamed veggies and ribs. She carried it to her table and took the dishes off her tray and put it to the side. She hated trays. They always made her think of cafeteria or fast food instead of real home-cooked meals. She walked back over to grab water and another pot of tea. While she was there, she eyed the desserts, not sure if she needed to take what she wanted now or if something would still be left when she came back. Colton walked up beside her with a plate that already had three or four desserts on it.

"Do you want more than this?"

She stared at it, her eyes huge. "Is that just for me?"

He shook his head. "For both of us."

She added a piece of pecan pie to it, and they traipsed back to the table. Everybody else ignored them and just let the three of them sit alone at their table, which could easily hold more. "Are people unfriendly here?"

Troy shook his head. "No, I think they're all busy dealing with stuff. Plus we're the outsiders."

She nodded. "That's how I feel too. Like an outsider."

"Don't let it get to you," Colton said.

She shrugged. "It doesn't matter. I just want to get home."

"I can see that," Troy said. "Any fear about flying again?"

It was a subject she had briefly wondered about and hadn't really given too much thought to. "No," she answered slowly. "I don't think so. I might like to do some more parachuting though, so I'm much less scared about the process."

"I'm sure you've done your training."

"Sure," she said with a half smile. "But it was years ago, and I haven't really maintained it."

"Training is only so good," Colton said. "It doesn't replace the real thing."

"No, it doesn't," she said. "It's trying to keep the emotions, the shock and the fear under control. That's what was so hard. When I saw that water rushing up, I knew I would hit and hit hard, but I was so afraid of drowning with the chute."

"Understood," Colton said. "It's one of the reasons I tried to get there as soon as I could."

"But then George was sinking."

"And his chute filled and sank on me too," he said. "They were too big to try to fill with air and use for floatation. If it wasn't for the temperature of the water, I might have been able to pull that off."

Kate shook her head, getting cold all over again. "It was all so shocking," she murmured, then looked down at her plate of hot veggies and attacked it. "And this is why I'm hungry," she muttered. Picking up a big piece of steaming broccoli, she started munching. "This is really good," she said a moment later.

"Smaller bases tend to have better food," Troy said in a low voice. "They don't have to cook for so many, so it's generally hotter and fresher."

"I don't know," she said. "I've been in all kinds of little bases all over the world, and it seems to me that there's a certain type of food, no matter what."

Colton just laughed at her.

"It's all good," she said with a smile. "I'm just happy to be here and able to eat."

"Good point," he said. "Keep it that way."

"What I would like to do is get answers though. Not knowing is hard."

"Not too sure we can do much about that," he said. "I'm afraid we'll get kicked out of the investigation."

"Maybe," she said, "but what about my ex, Ned? Maybe he had something to do with it."

"Maybe and then what?" he challenged her. "You go back to California and what?"

"I don't know," she said. "Try to avoid him, I guess."

"What if he did go so far as to bring down that plane? Do you think he is capable of that?"

"Can you ever know someone else and their thoughts?" she admitted with a sigh. "Yet, from what I saw, yes, I think so."

AFTER LUNCH, COLTON worked on his loaned-out laptop, digging into Kate's ex-boyfriend's life and calling in favors to get some of the military background he needed. Mason contacted him on a chat window and said that her ex-boyfriend had been picked up for questioning.

Claims he knows nothing about it.

Of course not, Colton replied. **Did he have opportunity?**

We do have him at the airport at the same time she was there, but then he's a pilot, so that's where he belongs.

What about the mechanics? Did anybody see him around there? Colton pushed for more.

Not that anybody is talking about.

Any best friends or family in the mechanics line?

Not that we've been able to find.

Damn.

Plus, the two men being court-martialed over the drug thing are both still detained.

Friends or relatives? Anybody like that close by?

Both have a brother, but neither of them were in the military, nor were they recorded on base.

Somebody would need military clearance or at least contractor credentials to get on or off the base.

Yes, Mason replied. **But we both have seen cases where they could get in and out a little easier than actually having clearance.**

Yeah, that's true. Colton stared off in the distance. **What about Halifax? Why did they fuel up there? That seems weird.**

Problem with the gas line.

Another attempt at sabotage?

It's hard to say. Did Kate mention it?

No, but another plane was down for a problem too. Both of them at Halifax. Plus a plane traveling with it landed too.

Interesting. But that's what planes do.

It does all seem awfully hit or miss. I'm probably just grasping at straws here, Colton said.

Maybe so, but the thing you may not realize is that this was the same plane George and Kate flew regularly. Just not always to this base.

How regularly?

Several days a week, Mason replied.

Is that common?

Because of the type of trips they did, this is the long-range plane that they took most of the time.

So really, anybody who wanted to set up something like that could have had it established a while ago and just needed the right timing to execute the plan, Colton proposed.

In theory, yes, Mason wrote. **But don't forget. Maintenance on these planes is pretty specific and thorough. A bomb or any kind of incendiary device should have been noted.**

Potentially, unless somebody there knew about it and was covering for Ned.

But there's not just one mechanic involved, Mason warned. **These planes are gone over by teams.**

Colton knew he was reaching, but there had to be an explanation. **Any chance the ex-boyfriend was on that plane downed in Halifax?**

I can check. Is there a potential Halifax angle for the other suspects?

Yeah.

So that's possible, and they could have been at Halifax too, right?

Possibly, but that was kind of a one-off. How do you set up something like that?

You don't always, but that doesn't mean it's not possible.

Again this sabotage seems like it was preplanned and very coldly thought out, Colton wrote. **Hardly an off-the-cuff thing.**

But it's not that impossible. How hard would it be to put something inside or outside of the wing? It doesn't have to be very big these days.

No, I guess not. Colton thought about that, wondering just what it would take to blow up an aircraft's engine under a wing. And what was the smallest thing that could set off a fire there. He started a Google search on that, when a shadow fell over his shoulders. He looked up to see the commander staring at his laptop.

"Interesting topic," he said. He sat down beside them at the table, waving off their movements to salute. Turning to Kate, he asked, "How is the statement coming along?"

She smiled. "I think I'm done, sir." She handed him two sheets of paper, fully covered in writing. He took a moment to read it, asking her some questions about her statement, then finally nodded, turned to the second page and said, "Sign it and date it, please."

She did just that.

"Perfect," he said. "I'll get it scanned in."

"Thanks," she said with a smile. "I guess I could have put it into a Word document or an email for you."

"This is fine," he said and looked back at Colton. "Any luck?"

"Not yet," he said, "and I'm a little frustrated by it."

"Of course you are. The trouble with sabotage is that it's pretty damn easy—once you figure it out."

"I know, but figuring it out is the hard part. Where was the opportunity? How long ago was something like this planned, and how did they manage to pull it off?"

He nodded. "I hear you, son. Keep digging. Just keep my men in the loop." Then he got up and left.

Colton looked at Kate and then back at Troy, one eyebrow up. "What was that all about?" he asked after the commander had disappeared out the door toward the hallway.

"I don't think the commander likes anything happening on his base without him knowing about it," she said. "So I'm thinking he wanted to see what you were up to."

Colton nodded. "Still, it was a little odd."

"Small base, very involved commander," she said. "Large base, more layers between the commander and the people."

And that was so true. He went back to his research, but his mind was caught up with *opportunity* now. He switched his research to looking up the smallest amount of C-4 required to blow up a plane's engine. He was shocked to see how little it was. Particularly if it was placed strategically.

What was even more bothersome was the fact that the instructions on how to blow up a plane were included. Or a car or anything else. As he kept going down the rabbit hole, he also learned it was easy to cover with something like duct tape to make it blend into the color of the engine. And, as long as it was relatively flat and had a small computer chip for remote detonation, it wouldn't have to be where someone could easily get to it. It wouldn't take long to attach, and, if so disguised and applied underneath, nobody would have seen it.

Which was probably what was done here. It would be impossible to prove at this point, but somebody had taken C-4 or another plastic explosive and had placed it under the wing or at least on the inside where it wasn't easily seen. It could have been attached with just a simple slap, something that could happen as two guys talked and wandered past. Of course, nobody was close to the planes except the people who needed to be, unless something odd was going on.

Colton frowned, then opened up the chat to Mason again, asking him to make sure there wasn't any media event or anything that would have brought strangers into the hangar where the planes are.

Already on it, Mason wrote. **I'm tracking the video feed from that whole area.**

I hadn't realized what a small amount of C-4 would have done the job, or how easily it could be applied and hidden.

And cover it in duct tape, right? We probably read the same article, Mason said. As these crooks are getting smarter, we have to be that much smarter ourselves.

Yeah, especially with the directions sitting on the internet. We don't need a suspect with special training now, just an asshole who can read.

CHAPTER 8

KATE STOOD AND said, "As much as I've enjoyed this, that big meal has made me very sleepy. I'll head back and have another nap. I'll talk to you two later."

With that, she headed out. She knew she'd surprised them, and both men were probably figuring out if they should follow her or not. She didn't care either way; she just wanted to go to bed and rest. Something about a big meal when she was already tired was enough to finish her off. She didn't want to screw up a potentially good night's sleep tonight, but she was too tired to keep her eyes open.

She also got lost twice but finally found her way back to her original bedroom and got into her room, noting that the hair Colton had placed was still there. With a sigh of relief she stepped inside and found the privacy absolutely wonderful. Kicking off her boots, she slipped under the covers, fully dressed once again. It wasn't long before her head hit the pillow, and her eyes closed.

The trouble was, she couldn't sleep. It was the same old, same old—realizing the engine was gone, the flames tearing off the back of the plane as it tilted and plummeted downward. In a death spin, they could do so little about it. It was hard to get up off that seat and get to the back, only to be caught by Colton and clipped into a harness and sent out the door.

She recognized that George had been treated the exact same way, and, for that, she realized they definitely owed Colton's SEAL training for their lives. But it was more than that; it was just Colton's cold sense of purpose. He didn't ask questions; he didn't worry about anything. He simply grabbed them, buckled them into their chutes and made sure they got out of the future wreckage heading toward the ocean.

It was her first major plane crash, and, even now, it hadn't really settled in. It was just too devastating. Too emotionally soul-destroying to walk away from. It didn't change the fact that she was a pilot and a damn good one, but she had to wonder if this would impact how she flew. She wanted to get back up in the air and get back down again safely several more times immediately, so she didn't have to deal with stage fright or whatever it's called when you didn't want to go back up in the air.

Flying was her whole life. She'd been wondering about settling down a little bit in the future and taking fewer shifts, but she had never wanted to give up the skies completely. It was a huge part of who she was. Yet sitting where she was now, it didn't seem to make any difference. She was curled up in bed, lost and caught in nightmares just so impossible to figure out.

What about all the equipment and cargo they were carrying? What were the chances that anything from the cargo bay could have been involved? Anything was possible. A timer could have been set inside the cargo that would have set off the engine as well. The bottom line was that either she or George had been targeted. It was also possible that it was all one and the same. Maybe the saboteur wanted both of them done for.

As shocking as that sounded, it wasn't out of the realm of possibility. All they had to do was find a connection between Ned and the guys doing the drug running. Ned had been volatile. He could be very up and then very down too. She now wondered if he took drugs. It would explain the mood swings. As she lay here, she tried to figure out some commonsense rationality about any of it, but it eluded her. Finally she got frustrated and sat back up in bed and groaned.

No point in resting here, if I'm not resting. But, if I can't rest, no point in letting my mind bend upside down and backward. But she had none of her gear, not even a laptop. She should have asked Colton if she could have taken his with her for a bit. Maybe it would have helped—if for no other reason than giving her something to do. Just as she got up and put her boots back on, a light knock came at the door. "Come in?"

Petty Officer Parsons stepped in, smiled at her and said, "I wondered if you were napping."

"No," she said. "I tried, but I've got too many thoughts going around in my head."

He nodded, then said, "The commander would like to have you check in at sick bay, please."

She stilled and then nodded. "I guess that makes sense, but I can't say that I want to." She finished lacing up her boots, then stood, walking toward him and asked, "Any chance you can show me the way?"

"I'd be happy to," he said. "The commander is just looking after your health."

"Maybe so," she said, "but it still feels very much like more poking and prodding that I don't want done."

"You have a fair bit of bruising, according to your file,

but no broken bones. That in itself is amazing."

She nodded grimly. "You can thank Colton for that."

"No, not just him, I don't think so," he said. "Maybe because you got out of the plane so fast, and he kept you alive in the water, but, all in all, the three of you did a great job."

"Maybe."

Suddenly they were in front of the medical center. With a smile she stepped inside, and he faded away. As she walked forward, a woman looked up and smiled, then asked, "Can I help you?"

"The commander sent me to report here for a checkup," she said.

"And you are?"

"I'm the one who just arrived from the crashed plane," she said. "It's Kate. Kate Winnows."

"Good to have you," the woman said. "Take a seat. The doctor will look after you in a moment."

That was the best she could do. She sat down but, of course, no magazines were here, like those found in most civilian waiting rooms. Nothing but windows surrounded her. She stared, realizing just what a unique country this was. When she started to get bored and looked for something to occupy herself, a big burly male stepped in and called her name. She hopped to her feet, then smiled and said, "That's me."

He looked at her, then said, "Well, the fact that you're walking, talking and appear to be quite sane already qualifies you as a miracle. Come in and tell me your secret."

She laughed at his humor, liking him already, and followed him into a small room. He did a very thorough checkup, asked her about all kinds of things she hadn't even considered but were obviously pointed toward the possibility of internal injuries.

When he declared her fit and sound, she smiled and said, "That's what I said, but the commander wanted me to come anyway."

"Doesn't matter," he said. "It's always better to get you checked over, just in case."

He tapped his tablet. "What I do want is for you to see a colleague of mine."

"Why?" she wailed, the smile falling off her face. "I don't see any point."

"Of course you don't. That's because you're not interested in dealing with it right now. But the fact of the matter is, I think you should talk to somebody about it. The point is to make sure that you don't end up with recurring nightmares and that the stress doesn't leave you with PTSD long-term."

Enough common sense was behind his request that she could see his point. "How about I see somebody when I get back home again?"

"How about you see somebody now?" he said firmly. "And I mean like *now*, now."

With that, he handed her a note and said, "Talk to my receptionist out front. With any luck you can go straight from here to your next stop."

Kate nodded glumly and said, "You know that's almost worse than getting blood taken. And I hate needles."

He gave a big laugh. "For anybody who survived what you did, talking about it should be a piece of cake."

"It wouldn't be bad," she said, "if they wanted to know something straightforward. But it's always those tricky questions where they're trying to read between the lines. That's the hard part."

"So then, say you just want to talk straight and don't want your brain analyzed while you're at it."

She looked at him in surprise.

He shrugged. "Why not? That's what I do. I have to go for mental health visits too, whether I like it or not. And like you, I don't like the double-talk stuff. I want, *This is where I'm at. This is what I'm doing. This is how I'm doing,*" he said. "You might try that."

The trouble with that strategy was, when it came to put it in practice, it was easier said than done.

She was surprised when she arrived at the shrink's office. Still a military office and plainer than she would have expected for a psychiatrist's office, but the beaming smile on the woman's face was the biggest surprise.

"I suppose he told you to ask for the no-frills plan," she said warmly.

Kate laughed out loud. "Only after telling him that I hated how you guys always look for answers inside the answers."

The doctor laughed. "I love it," she said. "But seriously, my only interest is ensuring that you are coping okay with the terrible experience you had."

"I'm okay," Kate said boldly. "As much as I want and need to sleep, the nightmares keep me up. I still see myself crashing but drowning instead of being rescued. I presume with time that will ease up."

"Yes," the doctor said. "You weren't hurt physically?"

"No. It was just a bad accident. I avoided the plane crash via parachute, followed by very nearly drowning, and then the hypothermia set in," Kate said with a laugh. "And thankfully I survived it all."

"Thankfully, indeed," the doctor said. "And I heard

from others that you've credited the man flying with you for the survival of you and the other pilot?"

"Yes, Colton," Kate said with a gentle smile. "No doubt about it. No way George or I would have made it without Colton."

"The two of you have a history?"

"A one-night stand four years ago," she said, clear-cut and concise. "I would love to explore the idea of a relationship, but I don't know that he's up for it."

"If he is," she said, "I can tell you an intense experience like this can make for a great bond. Nobody else will understand what you've gone through but him."

"But is that a fair basis for a relationship?"

"Is a one-night stand?" the woman countered, then followed with a big smile. "It's a great basis. It's like a sympathetic understanding with a lot of realism attached to it. Makes for reality and a relationship that is grounded instead of one built on fantasy. Fantasy is great, until you pull back the curtains and see what's really inside. In this case you already know the core of the man. You can create a beautiful world from that without any fantasy required."

COLTON SAT AT an empty table in one of the office buildings, doing his best to figure out exactly what the hell was going on. What he had were all kinds of details and various opportunities to sort out, but absolutely no information that would do them any good. And that was really irritating. He needed answers, but, so far, everything was coming up blank. Troy joined him a few moments later. Colton raised his eyebrows.

"I thought you'd be with Kate."

"She's napping," he explained. "I figured I could do better here, trying to get some answers in the meantime."

"There are definitely answers that need to be found, but I sure as hell haven't had any luck finding them."

"We have to track whoever was on the plane or in the area and compare them against our three suspects," Colton said. "At the moment, all three look good for this, but we haven't gotten anybody verified in position at the scene, so really there's no case."

"All have motive," Troy said, "but motive isn't enough."

"I know," he said with a groan. "Wish it was."

"No you don't, not really," Troy said. "The world would go crazy, pinning all kinds of crimes on the wrong people. Look at what a mess the world is in already. Can you imagine how much worse it would get without due process?"

"I know," Colton said grimly. "Okay, so I've got a passenger list from the other flight that had a mechanical problem and ended up at Halifax. Let's check all the passengers against our three known suspects."

"Give me half," Troy said, and, between the two of them, they broke it up and started covering all the names on the list.

By the time Colton got through his section of the list, he was frustrated to the point of swearing. "Damn it. Not only is nothing here, nobody even looks remotely connected."

"Nobody with any history of assaults or a criminal record flagged for anything at all?" Troy asked, looking up from his part of the list.

"Nothing," Colton said. "It's so freaking irritating."

"It is," Troy said. "There has to be some connection to somebody though. That plane didn't blow up on its own."

"I guess that's one of the things we have to consider—

the possibility of mechanical failure."

"It's possible, but, Colton, given the motives we've got here, it sure doesn't look all that probable."

"Right. In most investigations, you spend considerable time trying to find a plausible motive, but here we've got motive up the—"

"Exactly."

But with Troy's half of the passenger list now completed too, Colton couldn't do much more until he got a couple things from Mason. First, he was still waiting on Kate's contact list from her old phone. So he reminded Mason, who was waiting on the girlfriend's email containing snapshots of said contacts. He'd send that on upon receipt.

Now Colton had a second request, a new one, asking for the list of mechanics working on the base around the planes in the twenty-four hours before their flight took off, as well as verifying what kind of a visual check would have been possible in order to determine how long that bomb could have been sitting there, waiting to be triggered.

When he explained that, Mason had said he'd get back with it in a few minutes. Colton hoped he wasn't putting Mason on the spot over all this purported sabotage—which could have occurred at two other bases—but obviously something was going on. Having been caught by surprise once, Colton sure as hell didn't want to get caught a second time.

Minutes later, Mason came back on the chat window.

Ex-boyfriend is in the clear over Halifax. Confirmed he was in Colorado. Colton, did you ever consider you were the target?

Sitting up a little straighter, he looked at Troy. "Mason just asked if I might have been the target."

Troy's eyebrows rose. "Ooh, I hadn't considered that."

"But it is a possibility, I suppose. But how though? It's not like anybody knew I was on that plane."

"I did," Troy said. "And, if I did, you know a bunch of other people on base, *both* bases, did as well."

Colton frowned. "I wouldn't have thought I had that many enemies."

"You don't need many. All you need is one, one with the right skill set to do this."

"The trouble is, because we don't have the plane to investigate, we don't have a signature on the bomb or anything else for that matter," Colton said.

"In a way, it was a perfect crime," Troy said. "Except for one part."

"What's that?" Colton asked.

"You survived," Troy said. "If this was a murder-for-hire, the guy failed to complete the job, and he'll be coming around, looking for another opportunity."

"Oh, good. Just when this wasn't complicated enough."

"I'm thinking you better spend a few minutes and figure out who might have wanted to kill you."

Colton looked at him. "You know full well, because of the work I do, anything is possible, but I just don't think it's a likely answer."

"Maybe not but it's something we do need to mark off as having been looked at."

"Fine, I just don't like it," Colton said with a scowl.

"Like it or not," Troy said with a chuckle, "it's something that has to be considered and then either discarded or brought up for a further look."

Grumbling about that, Colton faced his borrowed laptop and sat here with a serious look, figuring out just who in his life might have wanted to kill him. And who he had told about his plans. "I told a couple of the guys," he said. "When I was sitting there, waiting for the flight out of Coronado, I was talking to somebody."

"You told him what you were doing?"

"To a certain extent but not with any detail."

"Did you know him?" Troy asked.

"I know *of* him, but I don't *know him*, know him," he said. "As in, he's not a friend, and I've never done a mission with him. At least I don't think so." He tried to recall the man's features, and then he shrugged. "I can't remember very much about him. It was just a casual conversation about how I was heading up to Greenland and that this was the flight I was put on."

"And where did you talk to him?" Troy asked.

"At the plane," he said. Looking at Troy, he repeated, "*At the plane*. That's the thing."

"Were they loading up supplies? Anybody who was involved in the loading there would have had access to the plane. If a bomb was attached to the outside, they could have just walked past casually and done all kinds of things."

"He was there alone," Colton said, quietly pissed at himself now for not having noticed.

Troy said, "Listen. The thing is, because he was right there where you expected to see somebody, it didn't seem like it was out of the ordinary."

"Not to mention it was on the base, where you assume everybody is okay." But, of course, Colton already knew from previous experience you couldn't assume anything. Shit happened no matter where, and sometimes it was worse on the base because everybody assumed it was all clear.

"He had to have been there with the group doing the

loading," Troy said. "At least he was somebody nobody had a problem with."

"True, and, since everybody else was calm about it, so was I. ... Then again maybe it looked like he was there with me."

"That's possible too."

Colton sat there a little longer and then sent a message to Mason, explaining that he had spoken to somebody at the Coronado airport himself. And he now needed a list of all the ground crew who might have loaded the gear onto the plane. "I suppose there also could have been triggers inside the plane. Like in the cargo as well," he mentioned to Troy as he worked.

"Instead of a phone call?" asked Troy.

"Yeah," he said. "It's possible. Anything's possible at this point."

"As usual there are too many possibilities. We'll narrow them down, and then, when we figure it out," Troy said, "whatever doesn't make sense and is still left standing, no matter how impossible, that will be the one lead we have to pursue."

Colton looked at him and smiled. "I've been spending more of my time doing training lately than investigations, you know?"

"Yep," Troy said. "Doesn't matter now though because, when it comes home like this one has, you'll do whatever you need to do to make sure you're clear and Kate stays safe," he said.

"We need to put a military guard on George too. Or a civilian one if we can't confirm the guards are clean."

"I wonder if anybody has considered that. You know it won't be well-received if we tell the commander he needs to consider a second attack."

"God, no, it sure won't," Colton said, "but we need to find out and deal with it."

Just then they looked up to see Petty Officer Parsons walking toward the cafeteria area, probably looking for a coffee. They hailed him over to the little office they were in, and he approached with a smile on his face.

"What are you two up to?"

"Just trying to figure out who might have been involved in this," Troy said.

"Right. Like the rest of us, you're trying to figure out if a crime actually occurred," he said with a laugh.

That gave Colton an idea just how much their word was doubted. "Well, there is a downed plane," he said quietly. "If nothing else, that should be cause for concern."

"To the number-crunchers and the supply guys, yes," Parsons said, "and obviously you guys. Plus, whoever's delivery was dumped in the ocean."

Colton hadn't really considered that angle. Somebody wanted that load shipped. Had crashing it benefited some-body else on a budgetary level? He hated to even think along that line, but, now that he had, it was one more thing to look into. When shit happened, it wasn't always easy to sort out who did the shitting. Again, there were no immediate answers. He faced the petty officer and asked, "Does George have base and civilian security on him?"

"I don't know, but I believe his condition is such that you could visit him at the hospital."

"Now that would be good," Colton said. "I know Kate really wants to check in on him."

"Let me know, and I'll arrange it." Then he headed over to get the coffee he'd come for.

"Something about him seems so nonchalant, as if he doesn't care," Troy said.

"I imagine a lot of them don't," Colton said. "When you think about it, the only ones who really care are those directly affected by it. To these guys, planes go down all the time, and, in this case, it was just a cargo plane with no loss of life. So it's an equipment headache. I was working my way through that angle in my mind, but I'm not really getting much of a hit on it being viable."

"Maybe it didn't have as much to do with killing George and/or Kate," Troy said thoughtfully. "Maybe it was as much to make it look like George was a shitty-ass pilot who shouldn't be flying or something. More to discredit him than anything else."

"But it's not like his preflight check would have shown up with something wrong in the engine or anything, not unless the computer revealed something."

"I suggest we talk to George," Troy said, "because you know that he's the one who would have the most answers."

"He also did the preflight before Kate was even there," Colton said thoughtfully.

"Are we thinking suicide?"

"That's a rough way to go," he said.

"It is, but we've seen it before."

"Well, I haven't," Colton said. "Wouldn't want to either. It's one thing if you take your own life but another thing to take others down with you. Besides, why would he want to do that when he has a wife and kids?"

"We don't know that everything's okay in the marriage," Troy said. "What if they were on the verge of a divorce or something?"

"Right, and a pilot may want to go down with his flight,

but would he want to take Kate too? Some people probably wouldn't want to fly with him because of the deal with turning in his coworkers."

"Although," Troy said, "since he'd gone that far into it and had taken all the heat he likely has, you'd think he'd want to stick around to see it through. Unless somehow he has left evidence behind and just doesn't want to be part of the zoo."

"Again, more thoughts I don't really want to consider," Colton said with a wry smile, "because it will be a zoo, going up against his own coworkers like that. And who knows what kind of crap George's been through because of it already."

"Exactly. That won't be fun for anybody. Including his wife and kids potentially. Maybe he thought this would be an easy answer."

"Well, it's time for me to find Kate. Then take a trip to the hospital and find out for sure."

CHAPTER 9

W HEN KATE STEPPED into the waiting room, she saw Colton walking in to greet her. She smiled up at him. "You don't have to follow me around, you know?" she said gently. "You saved my life, but—"

"And you saved mine. We've already been over that old ground," he said. "I came to tell you that we can see George, if that's something you want to do."

"Absolutely it is," she said with excitement. "He's that much better?"

"Apparently," Colton said. "We just have to tell the petty officer, and he'll arrange for us to get to the hospital."

"Can we go now?" she asked hopefully. He looked at her strangely. She frowned. "What?"

"Are you okay after all that? Do you need to rest or eat or something?"

"No," she said. "No more sitting around. I'd like to do something active. And definitely no more talking about my health or mental state, please!" she said.

"As long as all the talking needed has been done, and you're good to go," he said with a smile.

As they went to leave, the receptionist called back, "The doctor wants to see you in a couple days."

Kate froze, then looked at her and said, "I should be going home in a couple days."

"There's a good chance all flights will be canceled due to weather," the woman said. "In that case, she wants to see you again."

Resigned, Kate nodded and waited while the appointment was booked and thanked her. Then, with a smile, she walked out of the office.

"You don't sound so impressed. Was it terrible?"

"No, not at all," she said.

"Did she want you to relive the accident?"

"No, not really. I think she is just wondering how stable I am, mentally, in terms of returning to work. And, of course, any suggestion of me not being stable or not capable to return to work amplifies my own fears in that regard. That's just not something I want to deal with right now, thank you very much." She caught the surprised look on his face, and she nodded. "Of course I'm worried. It was a hell of a crash. I haven't been up since, and I wanted to go up right away, but apparently that isn't allowed."

"I think that's probably standard," he said. "You'll go back up when scheduled, the same as you always have, and you'll carry on just like the professional you are."

Her tone was lighter as she said, "Thanks for the vote of confidence."

"No problem. I'd fly with you anytime."

"You might be the only one," she said. "A certain aura attaches to pilots after you crash."

"Interesting," he said. "Meaning people don't want to fly with you?"

"Well, a crash doesn't exactly garner confidence, does it?" she said with a chuckle.

"I don't know," he said. "You survived. That should boost everybody's confidence."

"It doesn't work that way. But it's fine. I'll deal with it."

"Was this your first crash?"

"Yes," she said.

"Everybody has one bad experience," he said cheerfully.

At that, she burst out laughing. "Often you only get one."

"Point taken, but we made it out, so it's all good."

She loved his blasé, not quite careless, but almost, attitude. And really, the *It happened. It's over. Let's move on* way of thinking was not a bad way to go. Colton really was a good guy.

With great joy that they hooked up with Petty Officer Parsons, who arranged a ride for them and access into the hospital. It took a good twenty minutes to go from the base to where they needed to go, but very quickly they were inside the hospital and directed toward George's bed. He was sleeping. Kate hesitated, not wanting to wake him up. She looked at Colton to see his frown. "What's the matter?

"He was supposed to be awake," he said by way of explanation, but it wasn't enough.

"He's been through a lot," she said. "I'd be asleep too, if I could be."

At that, he nodded. "Right. Good point. And he was way worse off than you."

"Exactly," she said. "We can go get a coffee or something and come back."

"That sounds like a plan." Colton looked around and noted where the cafeteria was. "Come on. Let's go. We can always return and sit outside his room and hope he wakes up again."

She didn't like the way he said that. "You don't mean he might die, right?" she said, as soon as they were moving toward the cafeteria.

He looked at her in surprise. "No! No, that's not what I meant at all, but I have to admit to being disturbed at the fact there's no security on him."

"That's because nobody really believes it was sabotage. Accidents happen, fuel lines break, sometimes engines fail, and things overheat."

"Did you have any problems with the plane before that?"

"You asked that once before," she said. "I told you then it was a no."

"Were you awake the whole time?"

"No," she said, "I wasn't. I took a few minutes of shut-eye, and so did he. But nothing was unusual about that either."

"I know. Relax. I'm just looking into every angle I can," he said. "What is George's mental state like normally?"

She frowned. "Since the whole drug case, he's been a little morose, like he's almost sorry for what he started. He got involved and knew it was the right thing to do, but I don't think it's been easy. Not for him or his family."

Colton took a deep slow breath, and she watched curiously, realizing he was about to drop a verbal bomb on her. "Go ahead. Just tell me what's going on. Trust me. It'll be much better than not knowing what's going through your head because, honestly, you're kind of freaking me out."

"Okay, sorry. So you know we have to look at every angle, right? So one of the questions we have to consider is whether this could have been a suicide attempt."

Kate stared at him. "Oh, my God," she said. "Are you kidding? That is definitely not something I want to consider. I don't want to consider that at all."

"Maybe not but you know everybody else has to consider it. George got himself into a spot, and I'm sure his life hasn't been easy lately. Do you know if he and his wife were doing okay?"

"No, I don't know," she said, speaking slowly. "I know they had a temporary separation not all that long ago, but I can't imagine he would choose something like this. He loves those boys."

"What if he was sorry for dragging them into this mess? What if he regretted his actions and didn't see any way out?"

"But why would there be no way out?" she asked.

"I don't know. I guess that's something we have to look into." They walked into the cafeteria, and Kate picked up muffins and coffee. At least she thought they were muffins; they were a very unique-looking treat anyway. Colton paid for them, and they returned to George's room.

"Listen, Colton. I really don't like that suggestion. I don't like it at all."

"I know, but we've got to keep digging until we find something, somewhere," he said, as if trying to toss the idea back under the rock where he'd dragged it from.

"Do you have a way to check his email?" she asked slowly.

"Why?" Colton asked. At his sharp look, she clarified her question.

"I've spent quite a bit of time with George, and the only way he would do something like that was if his family was in danger. Like if he was being blackmailed into it."

"Oh, that's an interesting angle. I hadn't considered that." Colton pulled out the phone Petty Officer Parsons had turned up with at the request of the commander and contacted Mason. She could hear the conversation and heard Colton say, "I know it's a long shot, but—"

At that moment, she glanced at George, who didn't look very well. His face was turning red. She raced to his side and then hit the panic button. Alarms rang out; Colton jumped to her side. Almost immediately medical staff came running. Kate and Colton were ushered out of the room as medical staff worked on George.

Kate paced up and down the hallway. Colton looked at her and asked, "What happened?"

"He didn't look good," she whispered. From the doorway he joined her to look over her shoulder, trying to see. "I wondered if he was dying. I don't know. I just reacted."

"Yeah, especially if somebody was trying to help him along."

"I would go along with the murder and/or blackmail line," she said, "and both would be shitty options."

"True, but at least it would be him, not you and him," he murmured, his breath drifting across her cheek. Instinctively she leaned back into him, his arms coming around to hold her close.

They watched the medical staff fighting to save George's life.

He said against her ear, "I'll be right back. Stay here." And, with that, he dropped his arms from around her and headed off down the hallway at a rapid clip.

She called after him, "Where are you going?"

"To check the video cameras."

She stared after him in surprise and then realized how right he was. She didn't know what kind of credentials he needed to see them, but she was pretty sure he could pull whatever strings he needed to get the job done. With nothing else to do, she sat down and waited. With relief, she heard the atmosphere and the mood change inside George's room. She stepped up to take a look, and one of the nurses gave her a thumbs-up sign, a big smile on her face.

She crossed her hands against her chest and beamed. George had been saved. She didn't know what the hell was going on, but wow. "That was real shitty, whatever it was," she whispered quietly to herself. Two doctors walked out past her, and she asked the nurse, "Is he okay now?"

"For the moment," the nurse said.

"Do you know what happened?"

She shrugged. "His heart stopped. But he's back again."

Kate nodded and said, "Can I go in and see him?"

The nurse shook her head. "No, no visitors right now."

Kate looked at her and asked, "But what about monitoring him?"

"We've got him on the monitor at the nurses' station, and somebody will check on him every fifteen minutes."

Kate didn't like that one bit. "I'll just sit here for a bit." She sat down, picking up one of the coffees. She slowly sipped it, wondering how long Colton would be. Sure enough, the nurse came back, checked on George and gave her another thumbs-up as she left. That meant it had already been fifteen minutes. She waited and waited, and finally ate one muffin.

Still hungry, she ate the second one. She also drank Colton's coffee. By the time she saw him walking toward her, the nurse had come and gone once more. She bolted to her feet and ran toward him and threw herself against him. His arms closed around her, and he held her close. "It's okay," he said. "It's all right."

"It doesn't feel all right," she whispered against his chest. "Did you find anything?"

"It's what we didn't find. It took us a few minutes to get

clearance, but then, when they checked the security footage, they saw the system for this entire hallway was down for the twenty minutes we were in the cafeteria."

Kate stared up at him.

He nodded. "I know. Very suspicious."

"No," she said, "*deadly* suspicious."

"Exactly." He wrapped his arms around her and held her close.

IT HAD TAKEN a fair bit to get anybody to let him access the security cameras, but, when they realized what they had seen, orders were barked all over the place, and people had jumped in to try and figure out what was going on. Colton had stayed while they searched other hallways, looking for anybody who might have had anything to do with it, but, not finding anything, he decided it was time to go back. He sent Mason an update and then headed toward Kate.

The fact that there had potentially been an attack on George would hopefully bring the case up to a higher priority on base now that people had confirmation George was in danger. And that meant Kate was in danger too, only he'd left her alone. His footsteps rapidly increased until he almost ran down the hall. When he caught sight of her waiting for him, his heart slammed against his chest in relief. He shouldn't have left her alone. He never gave it a thought because she was surrounded by hospital staff.

When she'd seen him, she had raced toward him. It was natural for him to open his arms, and he was grateful she had jumped into them. He didn't know why the hell he hadn't tried to call her in all these years. He should have. Part of it may have been out of fear. That one night had been so good, and maybe it wouldn't be so good again. Foolish, he knew, but it was like one of those high spots in his life, and he didn't want to ruin it. And now his mind was completely overwhelmed with the fact somebody had managed to get into the hospital and to attack George—and could have attacked her too.

That meant it wasn't safe to leave him here. Colton hoped somebody was working on setting up proper security for George. Colton had passed on his own request, hoping it wasn't needed and that people were already working on it. But it was hard to know. His phone vibrated. Reaching for it, he looked down and frowned, then said, "Hello, Commander."

"Where are you?" the commander asked, his tone brisk.

"Standing outside George's hospital room."

"Good. Stay there," the commander ordered. "I have two men coming to stand guard."

With that, Colton let out a heavy sigh of relief. "I'm very glad to hear that, sir."

"The plane was one thing, but a second attack is another, although I don't know that I would have recognized it as such except for that damn security camera."

"Exactly," Colton said with a nod. "We'll stay here until the security arrives."

"When you get back," he said, "I want you in my office immediately." And, with that, he hung up.

Colton wrinkled his face. "Did you hear that?"

Kate nodded. "He doesn't sound happy."

"Doesn't mean he's unhappy with us. But the bearer of bad news has never been looked upon lightly," he said with a smile.

"Got it." Kate motioned at the empty cups and the paper bag beside it. "Your coffee was getting cold," she said, "so I drank it just in time." Enough laughter was in her voice for him to realize she hoped he wasn't upset with her.

"We can get more coffee and muffins," he said. "I'm glad we got as much as we did then. Obviously you needed it."

"I did," she said, moving back to sit down outside George's door. Just then a nurse came and entered George's room.

"We can't go in?" he asked Kate. "I was really hoping to talk to him."

Kate shook her head. "Every fifteen minutes they're doing checks, and apparently he's on a monitor at the nurses' station."

"Good," Colton said, "because the last thing we want is to have any other attempts made on his life."

"Or mine."

He slid his fingers through hers. Gripping her hand warmly, he said, "We'll make sure that doesn't happen either."

"Doesn't this prove it was just George they were after though?"

"Possibly, except they may be worried about what he or you saw."

Her gaze went wide. "I'd rather fly in the worst weather, in a damaged plane, over the worst enemy territory, rather than even *think* about people like that," she announced, shaking her head. "My mind doesn't work that way."

"No," he said, "but mine does, and the security team's does as well, so we'll do everything we can to keep you safe."

"That means you'll have to be with me all the time," she teased.

He gave her a special smile and said in a low whisper, "I plan to. Twenty-four hours a day."

"I'm supposed to be heading home tomorrow or the day after. Remember?"

"I hear you," he said, "but you're not getting on any plane without me and not before it's been checked thoroughly from top to bottom."

As her face paled, she nodded. "I appreciate that. I doubt I'll be the pilot."

"I doubt it too," he said calmly. "Not until you debrief back at Coronado. I don't know what kind of checks and balances they have to ensure you're fit to fly, but you can bet nobody will let you take the controls until it's cleared that you're as healthy as can be and that nobody is out to kill you."

"Somehow I feel like it's more likely about how I'm healthy and ready to fly than anybody is worried about me dying," she said drily. "Truth be known, the brass is probably more concerned about me keeping it together than anything else."

He laughed at that. "There are always jobs that nobody wants to do. That doesn't mean you have to suck it up and do it all the time."

"Maybe not," she said, "but George and I got along well."

"So George would have known you would be there this time too, right?"

She nodded. "Yep, he knew it."

"So any attempt to commit suicide would have been set up knowing he was taking you with him, right?"

"Yes," she said, her gaze curious as she watched him.

"So then most likely he wouldn't have been trying to

commit suicide."

"Except that he was really sad. Depressed even as we took off. So, I don't know, maybe that was part of it."

"It's possible," he said, "but let's hope not."

"What about his emails? Or any other way to check into his life to make sure he wasn't being blackmailed or something?" she asked curiously.

"There'll be a full investigation now," he said. "Whoever attacked him may have thought he would end things. But all he's done has expanded the inquiry, making sure it really does open up into a full investigation. So, this was likely the best thing that could have happened to George."

"A sad way to look at life." Kate's gaze turned to two uniformed men coming down the hallway toward them. "Looks like the security detail has arrived."

"Yes," Colton said. "Now we can catch a ride back."

"Is Parsons in town?"

"Or he'll come back to get us. I don't know."

As the two men approached, they said, "Your ride is waiting out front." Then they took up positions on either side of George's door. Kate wished she could see George one more time or at least let him know she was here, cheering him on, but it was obvious she wouldn't get close to George today.

With a smile she said to the guards, "Thank you for coming. Please keep him safe."

One of the men cracked a smile and said, "We will, ma'am. We will."

She didn't pull rank on them or mention anything other than the fact that it was important to her that George stayed alive. Colton appreciated that. At Colton's urging, she moved down the hall with him. She sighed as they took the stairs and headed out to the front door. "It's really sad," she said.

"What?" he asked.

"George doesn't know how much people are doing for him. I don't even know if his family has been told."

"That is up to other people. Remember? That part of the deal isn't something we can change," he said. "Unless you're good friends with George's wife?"

"I am friends with her. I used to talk to her every once in a while on the phone when George couldn't answer."

"Has that happened lately?"

"No," she said, sadness deepening her tone. "It hasn't."

.

CHAPTER 10

WHEN KATE AND Colton got back to the base, Kate thanked the petty officer for giving them a lift, and the three of them headed straight to the commander's office. Petty Officer Parsons stayed with her, smiling and saying, "He just wants me to keep an eye on you."

She shot him a sideways look. "For my protection or to make sure I don't run away?"

That had him laughing. "And why would you think that?" he asked.

"It hasn't escaped my notice I was there on the spot too," she said. The smile fell from his face, and he gave her a hard look. "Did you have anything to do with your copilot's attack?"

"Of course not," she cried out.

"Then you have nothing to worry about," he said. With a hard rap on the commander's door, they stepped in. The commander stood and motioned at the two chairs across from him. "Please, from the top."

Kate was grateful Colton did all the talking. When the commander looked to her, she nodded. "What he said."

He gave a clipped nod. "I want the two of you confined to the base, preferably to the cafeteria and your barracks."

Her smile fell off. "Why, sir?"

He shrugged. "For your own safety."

She wanted to kick up a fuss, but going against a commander on his own base was something likely to get her court-martialed. "For how long, sir?" she asked, desperately keeping her tone neutral, though she was heating up.

He grinned. "That cost you, didn't it?"

She gave a solemn nod. "You have no idea how much."

"Well, I'm glad you appreciate authority. Our forecasts shows some ugly fronts moving in. So, you won't be flying out for at least another two days."

She sighed. "Then you better add sick bay to your list of places that I'm allowed to visit. Your shrink wants to see me if I'm still here in a couple days."

"Good, I'll add that to the list," he said, then sat down and wrote a note. "I'll tell her that you'll be here for two more days anyway."

"Great," Kate muttered under her breath. He shot her a hard look, and she quickly added, "Thank you, sir." As soon as they were dismissed, her shoulders sagged.

Colton was at her side and said, "Come on. Let's go to the cafeteria."

"I'm still swimming in coffee," she declared.

"You are," he said with forced cheerfulness, "but I'm not."

She couldn't argue with that, so she nodded and headed that way. They'd missed dinner too. She stared at the staff already starting to clean up. She looked over at Colton and said, "I'm not *that* full."

He laughed. "Let's grab what we can."

They stepped smartly into the cafeteria. The chef looked at them and said, "Uh-oh, did you guys miss out?"

"Yeah," Colton said, "we were asked to stay over at the hospital until a security detail could arrive and relieve us."

"Tell me what you want," he said, motioning at the big serving platters, still sitting on the counter. "And we'll get you fixed up right now."

Kate opted for fried chicken and a huge platter of steamed veggies. With that, she headed for the desserts, even as they were yanked off the counter. She snagged two pieces of pie. With her tray full, she went to an empty table and set it all down, then went back for some milk, water and, as an afterthought, coffee. She knew Colton was making a quick round the same as she was. By the time they sat down, she could see most of the kitchen food had been removed. "Good timing."

"Right," Colton said with a big grin. "We could have been starving all night."

"Not a good thing for me right now," she said with a half laugh.

"How are you doing with the cold?" he asked worriedly.

She shrugged. "It was good timing for the coffee. Let's put it that way."

"Right. Well, let's hope you don't need to worry again for the rest of the evening."

Outside of the banging and clanging of the dishes and the conversation of the staff, they were alone in the big cafeteria, and Kate didn't mind in the least. She leaned forward and said, "Such a weird feeling being on a base like this and isolated in a way."

"But not deliberately," he muttered. His mouth was still half full, and he was plowing into his food at a faster rate than she was, but then she'd already had two muffins and two coffees recently. She picked up a piece of chicken and bit into it, then moaned. "I think fried chicken has got to be my favorite food."

"It would be a toss-up between fried chicken, steak, or lasagna for me," Colton said. Then he looked at her sideways and added, "And crawfish. Well, prawns of any kind."

"You mean, seafood of any kind," she said with a laugh.

"But prawns especially."

She really enjoyed spending the next however long it took for them to eat. They didn't race through the food, even though she knew the kitchen crew awaited their plates. She figured it could be the last load in the dishwasher, and, if two plates had to be done by hand, well, that was hardly a big deal. As they finished up, she pushed her plate to the side and moaned. "I want more, but I'm stuffed full."

"Good thing," he said, "because no more is to be had."

She smiled. "Do they eat all that's left themselves?"

"Possibly," he said, "or it could also be lunch tomorrow."

She brightened at that. "Okay, I'm down for that too." They sat here together, sipping their coffee and staring at the apple pie.

"So, you picked up two pieces," he said in a conversational tone.

She reached for both and tucked them closer to her. Then she grinned. "Were you fast enough to get any dessert?"

"No, apparently not."

"Oh, fine." She handed him one of the pieces. "I did think of you when I was picking this up."

"Sure you did," he said, but he snagged it anyway and drew it out of her own reach to his side.

She just laughed, really enjoying the kibitzing and joking back and forth. "It's hard to imagine," she said, "how much it feels like we haven't been apart for the last four years."

He nodded. "I was thinking that earlier today."

"It's like we're friends who just haven't seen each other."

He nodded again.

"Which," she said, "I would say we are."

"That works for me too," he said with a smile.

"I guess we just crossed into the friends-with-benefits thing back then."

"Considering we'd known each other for a couple years already," he said, "that would make sense too."

"And now we're not quite strangers, but we're not quite friends."

"We're definitely friends," he said in a much stronger tone than she expected. "The question is whether we're still friends with benefits." And then he waggled his eyebrows at her in such a comical move that she burst out laughing.

"Probably not a cool idea," she said, "given the current scenario."

"The scenario has absolutely nothing to do with it."

"You already said you're supposed to stay with me twenty-four hours a day. I don't want you to think that comes with benefits."

"Obviously it does not come with benefits," he said, his tone firm but friendly. "That has to be a mutual decision at the right time."

She was sorry she'd brought it up because it was obvious her comment bothered him. "I didn't mean to insult you. I know you would never take advantage and would never expect something like that."

"Good," he said, "because I would never want you to think that."

"No," she said. She looked down at her plate. She was done. "Did you make the connection that George being attacked in the hospital means that person is here on location?"

He picked up his coffee cup and nodded. "I was wondering if you had."

"I'm a little slow, but I did get it eventually." She looked around. "Does that mean it's somebody on the base?"

"I don't know," he said in a low tone. "But that's a line of inquiry somebody else will likely pick up, so we're probably better off to stay out of it."

"But you know we can't, right?"

He nodded. "And again, I was thinking that maybe it wouldn't need to involve you."

"You can't protect *the little woman* all the time," she said. "In my job I've taken an awful lot of shit just to earn enough respect from a lot of men to do my job."

"Not from me," he said.

"So don't treat me that way now," she said in a firm voice.

He sighed. "Is it wrong to try and keep you safe?"

"How is that keeping me safe?"

"If you start getting involved in this, you're putting your name and your face out front. That'll make you a target again."

"But, according to you, I'm already a target," she said slowly. "So the best answer really is solving this thing, so it won't matter who the target is. We've got to get to whoever is responsible."

"Yes," he said, "in theory. But that doesn't save your ass if it's on the line in the meantime."

"So ... what then? *You'll* investigate, and *you'll* keep me safe?"

"All while keeping you in the loop. How's that?"

She smiled. "That works. But you can't do too much investigating if you're stuck on a twenty-four-hour detail with me."

"Don't forget Troy."

She looked around. "Where is he anyway?"

"Pursuing the line of inquiry you just brought up."

She stopped and stared at him, her eyes widening. "Seriously?"

"Yes," he said. "We figured it was better that I keep you close, and that left him free to wander."

"What we have to know is who was not on base today."

"We know," he said in a soothing voice.

She glared at him, but he just grinned and said, "No, I'm not patronizing you, but I do want you to keep your voice down."

She winced as she realized her voice had, indeed, been rising. She sighed. "Put it down to hormones and emotions."

"How about just plain old stress?" he said.

She figured either he was avoiding any comment about hormones because she might have jumped up and bit his head off or he really did believe it was stress. As she thought about it, she had plenty to be stressed about. She just nodded and smiled. "I hear you. So now what?"

"Now," he said, "how about we go back to the barracks?"

"And?"

"My laptop is there."

She nodded. "Right and that's important too." She walked over to the counter with their dirty dishes and called out her thanks. One of the men poked his head out from the back and gave her a wave.

Following Colton, she headed back to the barracks. One

thing she could guarantee right now was that she was seriously tired. However, she also knew sleep couldn't be further from her head.

IT WAS HARD to walk a fine line between keeping Kate in the loop and keeping her out of things that Colton didn't want her to know. Mostly because he didn't want her to show any reaction to things he said to other people. And her face was so damn expressive. Hell, all of her was. One of the things he really remembered from their night together four years ago was every time they had made love—and it had been several times that night—she'd been so honest and open with her feelings and her response. He'd been completely enthralled, and he couldn't stop trying to make her enjoy herself even more.

And now that he knew for a fact just how expressive that face of hers was, she could never play poker because everybody else would know what she had for cards. That was why he had to play his cards close to the vest, but it was also a fine line. He didn't want to piss her off. Yes, keeping her safe was a priority, but she probably wouldn't hold it very high in her mind.

Her priorities were all about keeping George safe, which was admirable. And she also wanted to know who was doing this so they would be caught. She was right in the sense that it was the only way she could walk away from this and not look over her shoulder for the rest of her life.

As they headed toward the barracks, he looked at her and asked, "My room or yours?"

"It has to be your room. I've got a single bed. You've got bunks."

He nodded and didn't say anything. "Do you have anything in your room?"

"No, we moved it all last night, such as it is," she said. "I went to my old room today for a nap, and that's where Parsons found me." Colton opened the room and let her in. As soon as he got in, he sent Troy a text.

On my way, Troy replied. Colton motioned to the top bunk. "Troy is coming."

"Good," she said, as she stretched out on the bed. "If I fall asleep, don't wake me."

"Do you need a trip to the bathroom first?"

She could feel the heaviness washing over her. She groaned. "Yes, dammit." She made her way down off the bunk and headed to the bathroom. Since it was only a couple doors away, Colton stood in his doorway and watched. At a distance he could see Troy coming down the hall toward him. They stood close enough to have a private conversation in the hallway, the two of them talking as Troy brought him up to date. "I have a list of everybody who was off the base today."

"Was it hard to get?"

"I went straight to the commander and explained why we needed it."

"I bet that pissed him off."

"He was more pissed at the idea that somebody on his base, under his command, might have done something like this. He still doesn't believe it, and he is also interested in proving his men and women were solid and honest."

"That's an angle that works too," he said. "If all his people are clear, then it's not his fault."

"And it doesn't necessarily have to be anybody here either," Troy said. "There are way too many options."

"Not that many, surely," Colton said.

"I have about thirty-four names here, plus he added four names of men who used to work on the base but no longer do."

"No longer military?"

"One is on medical leave. Two are on dishonorable discharge. Another is off pending the outcome of an investigation."

"But not on the base?"

"No. Looks like they live in town."

"Interesting," Colton said. "I guess we have some work to do tonight."

Just then the bathroom door opened, and Kate walked out. She had scrubbed her face, the tendrils of hair around her forehead had curled with the damp water.

He motioned at her and said, "Come on. Time for you to get some sleep."

She smiled at Troy. "You missed the fun in town."

"Nope," he said, "I was having my own bit of fun."

She rolled her eyes at that. "Can't wait to hear."

"Unfortunately I didn't find anything," he said.

"What about people who were off base?" she asked.

"Yes," he said, "I've just brought a list. We'll split it up and start investigating."

"Perfect," she said. "You guys do that and let me know what you find."

At that, Colton chuckled. "As long as we keep you in the loop, right?"

"Absolutely," she said with a smile. "And, if I fall asleep, you can tell me when I wake up."

"Done deal," he said. Colton sat down, and he and Troy divvied up the work. Above, Colton could hear Kate's steady breathing settle out.

Troy stood and checked on her, then sat back down again and nodded, indicating she was asleep.

"Good," Colton said. "It's the best thing for her."

"Let's make good use of the next couple hours," Troy said.

"Seems like all we're doing is running down names," Colton said, after he accepted a sheath of papers from Troy.

"Yeah, in this instance, the commander also wants us to keep it very quiet."

"Of course he does," Colton said, and he opened up his laptop and started with the first name.

CHAPTER 11

WHEN KATE WOKE, it was bright in the bedroom. She rolled over to see Colton lying on the bunk below her, his laptop at his side, with sheets of paper beside him with scratches and notes all over it. His eyes were closed, and his chest rose and fell in a deep relaxed rhythm. She saw no sign of Troy. She slid off her bunk to the floor and opened the door.

"Where are you going?" came his sleepy voice.

"Bathroom," she whispered. "Just sleep."

"No way," he said. "Twenty-four-hour watch is twenty-four-hour watch."

She groaned. "I'll just go to the bathroom real quick." She stepped out, closing the door behind her. She made her way to the bathroom, used the facilities and then gave her face a good scrub. Oh, what she wouldn't do for some face cream and a good brush for her hair, not to mention her own favorite shampoo. As she made her way back, she saw Colton leaning against the doorjamb. She gave him a quick frown. "You didn't have to get up."

"Of course I did," he said with a smile. "Are you okay?"

"Yes," she said, "but I could really use a shower."

"That's easy enough to do," he said. "We do have a couple towels here."

Taking one, she headed back to the shower, not bothering to tell him not to wait for her because obviously he would anyway. He was such a sweetheart. She understood it was also his sense of duty, but she also really did appreciate it. When she was done, she came back out and could feel her body trembling.

"You don't realize," she said, "just how much effort it takes to shower until your body is knocked down with hypothermia."

"Pretty typical when you're exhausted," he said with a nod. He led her back into the bedroom, where she crawled up onto the top bunk. "Any chance of a change of clothes?"

"A bag should be coming in for you, with any luck."

"How can flights come in," she said, "if we can't get out?"

"I believe they landed in another city where the weather had already passed," he said, "then are driving it here."

"So, in theory, I could leave the same way."

He shook his head. "Not until you're given permission."

Cross, because he was right, she said, "Well, that flight better not be just for some of my clothing."

"No, it also brought some of the replacement supplies for those that got deep-sixed into the ocean."

She winced at that. "I don't even know what was on that load."

"It's kind of an interesting topic."

"Why?" She rolled over to look down at him. He was sitting up and leaned his back against the wall with the laptop on his lap.

"Just wondering if those supplies were part of this deal."

"I don't know what you mean," she said.

"What if he was trying to take them somewhere else?"

"George?"

Colton nodded.

"You're back to that him-being-blackmailed thing."

"Maybe," he said. "Grasping at straws, I know. But one theory has to work. There is an answer behind all this. It's up to us to find it."

"Maybe," she said. "Talking to George would be the easiest."

"Maybe we can do that today too," he said.

"What time is it?"

"It's 0730."

"Breakfast?" she asked hopefully.

He let out a barking laugh. "All you're doing is eating."

"I know," she said. "I wonder if I should see the doctor about it."

"No. It's stress, boredom, and you're still cold," he said. "I have to go to the bathroom myself, so I'll lock the door behind me."

"I think I'll be fine," she called out.

"It doesn't matter what you think." He closed the door behind him, and she heard a hard *click*. She groaned and hopped down. Loose papers were everywhere. She picked them up, studying the notes. Most of the men's names had been crossed off, but Colton had circled three with question marks. When he came back, she held up the papers and asked, "Did you find anything?"

"Hopefully today we will talk to two of the men who no longer work here. And we still have to talk to every one of these guys and get their whereabouts at the time the hospital security cameras went down."

She nodded. "I guess you couldn't do that overnight, could you?"

"Nope," he said cheerfully. "We were able to do background checks to see if anything suspicious turned up or if any connection was found to you or George."

"And was there?"

"No, nothing at all," he said. "But that doesn't mean they weren't paid to sabotage the plane for money, not caring who ended up hurt."

"Money does talk, doesn't it?" she said sadly.

"It does, but so does food." He looked at her smile and said, "Let's go and get you tanked up again."

She followed him down the hallway and said, "Where's Troy?"

"He'll meet us at the cafeteria." As they walked into the mess hall, Troy was already sitting in the far corner at a table, and he raised a hand in greeting. Kate smiled at him and grabbed a tray and a plate and looked at the selection. Everything from carbs in the form of waffles, pancakes and potatoes to eggs and all kinds of breakfast sausages were here. She looked at it and said, "Very American, huh?"

"A few traditional items from are also offered," Colton said, "but I definitely want an American breakfast this morning." He proceeded to load up on potatoes, sausages and eggs. Then he added hot buttered toast and walked toward Troy. She followed suit and then went back and got orange juice and coffee. Troy looked at their plates in approval. "Particularly when you're shut in for the weather," he said, "everybody eats so much more."

"I feel like, as soon as I eat," Kate said, "I'm hungry again."

"It just means your body is burning it up, and that's a good thing, from a healing standpoint."

Kate took a quick bite, then said, "I'd love to go back into town and see about visiting with George today."

"It's on the agenda," Troy said. "As soon as we're done eating, we're going in with Petty Officer Parsons. He'll drive us around as we need it."

"Good," she said. "That would be nice. The idea of being confined to the barracks, the cafeteria and sick bay was kind of freaking me out." As they went through breakfast, the conversation remained quiet and neutral. Enough noise surrounded them; they couldn't really talk without shouting to be heard. Kate just wanted to leave. When they were finally ready, they headed toward the front parking lot of the base, where they waited for Petty Officer Parsons to arrive.

When he arrived, he smiled, held up his briefcase and said, "I have a few errands myself, if that's okay with you guys."

"It's fine," Colton said. "Even better would be if we could have our own set of wheels."

"No can do," Parsons said. "The commander wants to know where you guys are every step of the way."

"Of course he does," Kate said with a smile.

Parsons looked at her with a questioning expression.

She just smiled and said, "It's only natural because he's responsible for everything that happens on the base."

"Exactly," he said. "There is good news in that a shipment with some of your stuff is coming in tonight."

"That would be great. What are the plans for today?"

"I'll drop you guys off at the corner by the park," Parsons said. "After my errands are finished, I'll pick you back up. These guys have all your stops for interviews mapped out."

Hearing that, she looked at Colton in surprise. "No MPs to follow us?"

He just shrugged.

"It's not a very big area. Can we just wander around and talk to people?"

"Yep, pretty much," Colton said. He didn't explain how they got clearance to walk around alone though.

"And attract all kinds of attention?"

"We would be in a military vehicle otherwise, so what's the difference?" he said.

At that, she acknowledged the point. "Fine," she said, and, sure enough, they were dropped off at a small park. She looked around and smiled. The weather was crappy, and it would obviously only get worse, but she could still appreciate being outside and being in the location they were in and how very unique it was. The place wasn't so much desolated as it had been a hard-fought battle to establish a civilization here. But once that battle was won, the people were a hearty lot. Parsons drove away, and she looked at the two men. "Where do we start?"

Troy pointed at Colton, who pointed at the closest house. "This one."

He walked up and opened a conversation, saying they were involved in an investigation on the base. Where had so-and-so been at such-and-such time. Did they know or have any connection to George and/or Kate. But never did they refer to her as being Kate. She found that interesting, as was their technique. The questioned men inevitably shook their heads, said they knew nothing, had been home or shopping or otherwise had alibis. The alibis were written down to be checked later.

Colton and Troy looked from one to the other and then at her, but, as nobody volunteered any information, there wasn't a whole lot they could say. When the questioning was done, Colton looked each man hard in the eye and said,

"Any discussion regarding this matter will require an immediate visit to the commander. You are to tell no one we were here."

Each man investigated nodded. "Understood." Each man saluted, and Colton nudged Kate down the stairs again.

"Do you really expect them to say anything different?" she asked, after they were heading down several more blocks.

"No, but if we catch someone in a lie," Troy said, "it's a completely different story."

She wondered about that and said, "You mean, after you check the alibis?"

"Yes," he said, "and I've been checking as we walk along." She'd heard him on the phone a lot but hadn't realized what he was doing.

"Do you think they've contacted their alibis already?"

"Checking their phone records afterward will be the next thing," he said.

"Ah," she said, "right. And, if they have disobeyed an order, not to let anybody know about our visit—"

"Exactly, and the commander will be very interested to have a personal talk with them. It doesn't mean they're involved in any of this, but it does mean their behavior is questionable." Colton smiled at her. "See? You're getting the hang of this."

She shook her head and said, "You're certainly wearing off my breakfast. So, where to next?"

"To see one of the men who lives in town who no longer works at the base."

"Why not?"

"He's pending an inquiry, and he married a local girl."

"Interesting," she said. When they got to the house though, nobody was there. As in nobody. No wife, no one.

They went around to the back of the house, and no sign of life was there either. When they came back around to the front, a neighbor stood glaring at them. "Who are you, and what are you doing snooping around Andy's place?"

"We're from the base," Colton said, his voice hard and authoritative. "When did you last see him?"

The man stepped back, flustered. "Um, not yesterday." He shook his head. "I'm not exactly sure. A couple days ago maybe."

"Do you look after his place when he goes away?"

"He hasn't been going away," he said.

"So do you have any idea where he is now?"

"No," he said, bewildered. "What's this got to do with anyway?"

"An official military investigation," Troy said, not allowing for any further talk or argument. He picked up the phone and made a call, while Colton thanked the neighbor and said, "Now please, go inside and close the door."

But instead the man turned belligerent. "If something is wrong in this town, I want to know about it."

"Interesting," Colton said, pulling out his pad of paper. "What is your name and phone number? And where do you work?"

The man hesitated but finally answered the questions.

"Thank you," Colton said. "We'll be in touch." He turned and looked at Troy, who nodded, and they walked back up to Andy's front door. Opening the screen door, they checked the front door. Finding it unlocked, they stepped inside. Immediately Colton stepped back out and turned toward Kate. "I want you to stay right here."

"Why?" she asked. He just gave her a hard look. She nodded. Seeing a chair on the front porch, she sat down.

"I'll be just inside the door," he said.

She nodded, the neighbor still standing there, his arms across his chest, now more curious than anything. She sat and waited. It took them ten minutes, though they did come to check on her several times. She didn't imagine anybody would be there. But before the men came back outside, the local police pulled up front. They got out and headed up the stairs. Kate opened the door to notify Colton, and her nose was assailed by a smell. She called out, "Colton, the police are here."

The neighbor took one look at the police and backed up to his property. The police shot him a look and made a motion for him to back up even farther. At that, he went up to his property and sat on the porch to watch. When the police came up the steps to Andy's house, Kate smiled at them and said, "Hi."

"And you are?"

She identified herself and then said, "Troy and Colton are inside."

"They better not be," the second officer said.

The wooden door opened, and Colton said, "Of course we are, but we haven't left this room."

"You reported a body?"

"Yes."

The cops stepped inside.

"You'll need something to cover your feet if you're walking through here," he warned them. Colton held out an arm, and she ducked under it to take a better look and gasped. He looked at her, nodded and said, "Please, just go sit back down."

She complied. The whole floor was covered in blood. She figured they'd found the man they were looking for, or his wife, she wasn't sure.

When they finally stepped back outside, she looked up at him. "Was it Andy or Andy's wife?"

"It was Andy," he said, "and he was shot in the head."

"Ouch," she said. "That was a lot of blood."

"Yes, it wasn't a very good shot. He didn't die immediately."

"That's even more awful," she said, gasping.

"It is," he said sadly.

"Are we connecting this to the base?"

"It's definitely something we have to look at."

"What about his wife?"

"According to his cell phone, his wife was visiting her mother on the other side of town."

"Interesting," she said, "so she hasn't been home yet."

"No," he said. "We'll go there next."

"No," the officer said behind him. "This is our case, and we'll take it from here."

COLTON NODDED. THEY had crossed into a different jurisdiction here, but, as soon as he had a chance, he'd contact the base and see what the commander wanted to do. As they stepped down to the sidewalk, he already had his phone in hand. When the commander answered, he explained the problem.

"Shit," he said. "I'll contact the police chief." And he hung up on him.

"Well, he's efficient," Colton said to Troy. "But not so good with explanations. He didn't say if he wants us to stay and work this or if it would just revert to a police investigation."

"I suggest that, before we run out of time," Troy said, "at least one of us heads off to the last three names."

"Let's stick together," Colton said. "And then we'll hear what the commander has to say." With that, they quickly and efficiently went through the last few names. But no surprises were had, and, of course, nothing but more alibis came. As they returned to the house with Andy's dead body inside, they saw a forensic van and more cops. Just as they approached, Colton's phone rang.

"You can go to the hospital now to visit George," the commander said, his voice sounding tired. "The police chief has taken over the investigation, but he'll keep us in the loop."

"Good enough," Colton said, "I would like to know if the wife has been found alive and safe."

"That I can confirm," he said. "Did you get a look at the bullet wound?"

"Yes," Colton said. "And, yes, it could easily have been army-issued."

"Of course." And the commander hung up on him.

On that note they headed toward the hospital. Colton pulled up his GPS and said, "It's about a mile to walk there." He looked over at Kate. "Are you up to walking, or do you want me to call for a ride?"

She shook her head. "A walk would be good. Something to shake off some of that heavy emotion."

"I get it," he said. "Let's go."

He exchanged hard glances with Troy. All this did was bring up more questions. What they needed to do was find a link back to either George or Kate. As they walked toward the hospital, they compared notes. "Absolutely nothing is here," Troy said in frustration.

"It could be a website or something, like a murder for hire?"

Both men turned to look at her. She shrugged. "I don't know. Maybe the best answers will come from George himself."

"Maybe." Colton had his doubts though. Too much was going on that they didn't know about. He knew the answer would be simple, and they just had to dig deep enough to find it.

"Did you guys get into George's emails?"

"Coronado is checking that," Colton said. "So far I haven't had any answers."

"Poke Mason again," Troy said.

Colton nodded and pulled out his phone and sent a text.

"What did we ever do without a cell phone?" Kate said, watching him.

He smiled and said, "I'm sorry that we don't have one for you."

"I presume the commander gave you one?"

He nodded. "It's a burner phone."

She nodded. "I hope somebody told my family that I'm alive and well."

"I believe Mason took care of that," he said. "He contacted your girlfriend anyway. She would have done the rest, I presume."

Kate nodded. "Not that they would have known there was a problem. I doubt the plane crash even made headlines."

"Do you ever look at the manifest or check over the cargo?"

"No, only if there's a problem," she said. "The manifest is checked over by the ground crew, then loaded and secured, and we just fly it from point A to point B."

"You don't get to know what's in it?"

"Don't get to know, don't get to argue, don't get to refuse," she said.

"Right, so military."

She laughed at that. "Isn't it always?"

"Minions are supposed to do as told, to not question, ours is not to know the reason why," Colton misquoted badly.

She nodded. "Are you really thinking maybe it was supposed to go somewhere else?"

"Maybe. And when George passed the point where they realized he wasn't following the new route, they blew it up. It's a theory." Colton shrugged. He wasn't sure it was the right one, but this was a process that wouldn't end until they found the proof to take them in the right direction.

"Well, somebody needs to get out there and start diving for that then."

"If we get proof that's what was going on, they will," he said. "But, until that point, it's an expensive recovery operation to avoid if at all possible."

She nodded and didn't say anything.

Up ahead Colton saw the large hospital. "Still a few blocks, but that looks like it up there." And he pointed.

She nodded. "Sounds good," she said, wrapping her arms around herself. "There's a definite chill to the air."

"I'll go past saying there's a chill to saying there's a real bite."

She glanced around. "Doesn't it feel like we're being watched?"

"I imagine everybody in town is watching," he said. "We're strangers, and now they've heard about the murder."

"Surely not," she asked, horrified.

"Oh, I'm pretty certain their great friends are well and truly on to this one by now. Andy's neighbor was mighty interested."

"True," she said sadly. "Everybody likes a good story, don't they?"

"Wonder if Andy had anything to say?" Troy asked.

"We'll never know now," Colton replied.

She nodded.

Finally they came to the hospital. Colton opened the front door, and they all walked in. At the reception the woman looked at him, smiled, nodded in recognition and said, "Last I heard he was awake."

They nodded, and Kate asked, "Do you know an Andy? Used to be at the base?"

She nodded. "I heard about something happening at his house." She lowered her voice. "Is it true he's dead?"

Kate nodded and whispered, "Do you have any idea who might want to kill him?"

She shook her head. "No. He hung around with a rough crowd some of the time. You know what I mean? A little bit of recreational drugs and stuff, but I don't think it was anything major."

"Any idea who we could ask to find out more?"

The receptionist looked down the hallway both ways, then grabbed a little scratchpad and wrote down a number. She slipped it over. "Don't tell him where you got it."

"I won't," Kate said with a beaming smile and turned to join the men.

"That was smooth," Troy congratulated her.

She handed over the number. "Figured we might as well figure out what kind of a person Andy was."

"True." As they walked forward, Colton dialed the number. When a voice answered at the other end, he said, "Hi, I'm a friend of Andy's."

"What about it? Are you looking to score too?"

"Maybe," Colton said. "I just don't know the town very well. I wouldn't know where to meet up."

"Where are you now?"

"Just around the hospital."

"Meet you out in the parking lot in five." Then he hung up.

"Shit," Colton said. "This guy wants to meet in five out in the parking lot." He glanced at her and then over at Troy.

"Take Troy," Kate said. "There's one dead guy already. I'll go sit with George."

From where Colton stood, he could see George sitting up in bed with a cup of tea. He nodded. "Don't leave this room."

She smiled. "Go before you miss your appointment." She walked in toward George and smiled at him. The two men turned and headed for the elevator.

CHAPTER 12

A S KATE WALKED in, she smiled at George, who looked so much better than when she'd seen him last. "There's a sight for sore eyes."

George's beaming smile flashed. "Didn't think I would pull through. Looks like I'll keep most of my fingers too." He held up his hands. Two fingers were bandaged and looking pretty rough, but the others were fine.

"Toes?"

"I'll lose most of them," George admitted. "But I'm alive, thanks to you guys."

"It was pretty touch-and-go," she said with a smile. "Honestly I wasn't sure I would make it either."

"That ocean," he said. "Man, was it ever cold."

"A full-scale investigation is going on into what happened."

George rolled his eyes at that. "Good luck."

"Meaning?"

"Meaning, nothing." But something cagey was in his voice.

"Will their investigation do no good?"

"No idea." But his gaze slid to the windows.

"Did you have anything to do with it?" Kate asked quietly.

He turned and looked at her, startled. "What do you

mean?"

"I'm asking if you were trying to commit suicide."

His eyebrows shot up. "No," he said. But his voice broke. He glanced at the doorway, where a nurse was coming in. She checked his temperature and his blood pressure, then clucked like a mother hen and disappeared.

"Are they still coming in every fifteen minutes?"

"They're coming in too damn often as far as I'm concerned," George muttered.

Kate walked closer until she stood right beside him. "What's going on, George? We can't tell if you've been blackmailed, if you were following orders or had ditched orders, or you were trying to take us all out with you."

He shook his head. "I don't want to say. Enough people are in trouble over this already."

"Someone's dead now," she said and filled him in on Andy.

"It's related?"

"I don't know," she said, "but it seems too coincidental not to be." Then she stopped, looked at him with a smile and said, "You don't know you were attacked here, do you?"

His eyebrows shot up as she explained about their last hospital visit.

"Holy crap," he said, reaching over and grabbing her hand. "What about my wife? My boys!" His voice was suddenly demanding and hard.

"I don't know. I would presume that somebody—"

George abruptly let go of her and sank back, but she could see he wasn't in any way at peace.

"I need to get out of here," he snapped, trying to sit back up again. "I have to find my family."

"Is your family in danger, George?" she asked, pulling

his hand back.

He stared at her with anguish in his eyes.

"Tell me," she cried out. "We can't fix it if we don't know what we're supposed to fix."

"I should never have done it," he said. "If I hadn't turned in my coworkers, my life would be normal, and I'd be happily looking toward retirement." So much pain was in his voice, as if this was tearing him apart.

"So what happened? Was somebody pressuring you?"

"They wanted me to stop," he said. "They threatened my sons. Said they wouldn't make it home from school one day, and I'd never know when."

"And what were you supposed to do? Withdraw your accusations?"

"I tried to recant. I did try," he said, "but the military wouldn't let me."

"And then what?"

"The blackmailers said I had to bring this shipment in here—drugs for Greenland. But I didn't dare. Because, once I did, then I would be just as guilty as they were," he cried out in agony. "How can people be like that?"

"Did you ditch us into the ocean?"

"Kind of. But I wasn't trying to kill us. I was hoping to come in for a crash-landing, and that would get us out of it and would burn up the cargo," he explained. "But it went badly."

"What did you do?"

"It's pretty easy. I just put some C4 inside the engine and triggered it from the cockpit. Only I used a bit too much. I'd hoped to bring the plane down, not have it blow up mid-air. I had a burner phone set to call yours to trigger the blast. It was in my pocket, all I had to do was push the talk button."

"Oh, my God," she said, staring at him. "You could have killed all of us."

"I wouldn't have done it if I wasn't desperate, and if I didn't think I could crash land close to the base," he said quietly, "and if I wasn't terrified for my sons and my wife."

"So, if they couldn't make the runs, then you were going to?"

"Yes," George said. "Didn't you ever wonder how I ended up taking over this run?"

"Since we were both new on the run at the same time, I wasn't really thinking about it. But I guess it was after you turned them in, wasn't it? What happened to the guy who I replaced on that fateful flight?"

"No clue. He called in sick. And yes," he said. "The thing you don't understand is that somebody here on the base is involved."

"Well, somebody local," she said, "was having a heyday attacking you. They actually took out the security cameras in the hospital so we'd have no idea who it was."

George fretted in bed. "That means I'm not safe," he said. "And, if I'm not safe, my family isn't safe either."

"We'll make sure your family is safe, and then we'll make sure you are too." Kate sat back for a moment. "Did you realize you were tearing apart my life? Colton keeps wondering if it was somebody I knew."

"That ex-boyfriend of yours is a piece of shit," George said, "but nothing like these guys."

"The two being charged aren't even on active duty, and I was told they're in custody and have been for weeks," she said. "So who else are they working with? And how are they communicating?"

"They used emails and mail and text, all kinds of ways," he said with a wave of his hand. "They could be working with anyone and everyone. It's likely a big operation and easy enough to cut ties with a few to keep everyone else safe."

"Like you?"

"Yeah, like me," he said. "I just couldn't do it though. I kept thinking about my sons and all the young men like them here on the island."

"Why Greenland, I wonder?"

"They were trying to stay under the radar, so to speak," he said. "Then they moved the drugs from here."

"Jesus. You'd think they'd fly into Germany."

"Sure, but the base here is much easier to get things in and out of. It's a small island. Nobody would ever think of it as a major drug center."

"Of course not," she said, "we don't even know how *major* is major here."

"All that cargo," he said. "I'd bet at least 50 percent of it was hard drugs."

Kate sat back with a *thunk.* "That's not good. And chances are, if they are doing that here in Greenland, they're doing it other places too."

"That was the impression I got. I don't know where it goes from Greenland, but it goes. A big population isn't here, so I highly doubt too much of it gets sold here. But all they have to do is get it to one of the major centers, and then, of course, the whole world is their oyster."

"Unbelievable." Kate sat there, not sure what to say. "The blackmailers would check your emails too, I bet. Trying to make sure you were toeing the line."

"Good," he said. "The emails will back up what I'm saying."

"But we still have to keep you safe." She looked around and said, "You don't even have any clothes here, do you?"

He snorted. "No. Not likely. I think they cut everything off me on the navy cruiser."

"Yes," she said, and then she thought about the other ships that called this base home. "They could have even moved drugs in through them and other ships."

"Anything is possible," he said. "Even small planes fly out from here. I mean, it's pretty easy to start moving it in different locations, once you break it down. The hard part is getting in a big shipment, and we just delivered it."

"Yeah, but we delivered it to the ocean," she said. "Hopefully it'll be thoroughly ruined, and nobody can salvage it."

"I'm not sure it's safe to leave underwater though," he said. "It probably poisoned the ocean."

So much bitterness remained in his voice that Kate reached out and stroked the back of his hand. "Remember why you did this," she said. "Keep your boys in your mind."

"I get it," he said. "But I'm not out of danger, and neither are you."

Kate sat back and said, "And here I was thinking I wasn't in danger now."

"No," he said. "Because you were with that shipment. If I go down for transporting drugs, it'll mean you go down too."

She wrinkled her face up at that. "I didn't know anything about it."

"Where's Colton?" George asked, suddenly frowning. "He survived, didn't he?"

"Yeah, he's fine. That cold water didn't seem to faze him. He's here at the hospital with me."

"Thank heavens for that. I thought I heard him onboard the cruiser, but I don't even know that I asked about him."

Such shame filled his voice that she just smiled. "Hey, George. You need to look after yourself now. It's a mess."

"It's a bigger mess than you know. This is a military mess …"

"One who was military but more recently a civilian was just shot."

"Right, Andy," George said. "And I doubt he'll be the last one before this is cleared up."

"The commander will sure be pissed when he finds out what's been going on under his nose. He'll get to the bottom of it."

"That would be good. Somebody sure needs to."

Kate looked around, wondering where Colton was.

"Are you waiting for Colton?"

"Yeah. They went to meet a friend of Andy's, somebody who is dealing drugs." She slid George a sideways look. "Sound familiar?"

George winced. "Let's hope they do more than just meet him because somebody needs to get to the bottom of all of this, and fast."

"Yeah, you're right there." Kate got up and walked to the hallway, looking up and down, but she saw no sign of Colton yet. She turned back to George. "Are they feeding you?"

"Yes, I don't want for anything. I'm fine. I'm healthy. I'll make it," he said firmly.

"I'm glad to hear that," Kate said with a big smile. "Now I need you to survive." She opened up all the cupboards in the room, but she found no clothing for George. Frowning, she said, "We'll have to get you some clothing from the base."

"That would be good," George said. "I mean, if I'm under attack again, I'll come out buck naked if need be, but I'd feel more comfortable if my Johnson was covered."

At that, Kate burst out laughing. He grinned at her. "Let's see if I can find anything here. Maybe in the lost and found."

"Okay," he said, "maybe ask at the nurses' station."

Kate headed down the hallway to the nurses' station. She found a receptionist or maybe a head nurse. She didn't know; she didn't understand the uniforms here. She asked if there was any clothing for George. When the woman understood the question, she frowned, shook her head and said, "Only what he came in with."

"Which was nothing unfortunately," Kate said.

"Let me check the lost and found." She came right back with a large black bag, saying, "This is all we have."

"May I take it to his room?" Kate asked. "That way we can see if anything will work for him."

She nodded. "Bring back what's left when you're done."

Kate took the bag to George, still lying in bed. "We've got this to work with," she said, holding out the bag. Carefully she dumped it on top of him. And, between the two of them, they managed to find a T-shirt and a pair of shorts. They found no underwear and no socks for him.

"Well," he said, as he looked at his toes, "I won't have much to cover soon anyway."

"You won't be running for a while, but this will give you something to wear, just in case." Kate piled everything back into the black bag. "If you're good with the T-shirt and shorts, I'll take the rest back."

"That's fine. I don't know what happened to my underwear. You'd think they would have left those on."

"I know, right? We'll get you some from the base. This is only in the case of emergency."

"Let's hope it doesn't come to that," he said with a heavy sigh. "But you're right, it gives me something. Not very much but enough that I could make a run for it, if I have to."

"You need to try walking first," she said with a nod to his damaged feet. "You may very well find you can't run for your life."

COLTON AND TROY ran down the stairs, choosing that over the elevator, and bolted out the back door to the parking lot. As soon as they hit the lot, they separated, with Troy going to the shadows to keep an eye on Colton and his meeting. Colton, not knowing who he was looking for or where he would find him, headed toward the far end of the lot, figuring anybody looking at a drug deal would stick to the shadows. But he couldn't guarantee that.

As he'd come to learn, many people working in the world of drugs were fine upstanding citizens with reputations that kept them front and center. But they weren't always the most forthcoming about their drug habits. And they always had dealers in the background. As he walked all the way to the back, he saw no sign of anyone. He leaned against the cement wall and crossed his arms, keeping himself visible, just in case. He could see Troy moving between the vehicles up ahead. When a sound came from his left, he glanced casually over to see a male of around fifty, standing with his hands on his hips, his eyebrows raised.

Colton raised his eyebrows and looked directly at the

man. "Hey."

"No fucking *hey* with me," the dealer sneered. "How did you get my number?"

"Off the phone," he said. "You want to talk drugs or no?"

The guy looked around hurriedly. "What the hell are you, suicidal? None of this is brought out in the open."

"Andy was pretty verbal about it."

"Andy was a fucking idiot," the man snapped. "And, if you're thinking I haven't heard he's dead by now, you're wrong."

"Good," Colton said. "Then we're on the same ground."

"And what ground is that?" the dealer asked suspiciously. "And why the hell did you contact me? You don't look like a user."

"No, but I might be a supplier."

An odd stillness came over his face. "Shit," he said, glancing around. "The plane went down, I heard."

"It did," Colton said quietly. "And, yes, the cargo was lost."

"It was a dummy run anyway," he muttered.

He spoke just barely loud enough for Colton to hear. His eyebrows rose. "Interesting," he said. "Three people almost died on that flight."

"Yeah, I heard," he said.

"Interesting gateway."

"Coming in from the north, nobody else expects it, but an awful lot of the population lives within just a few hundred miles. Much less regulation and a lot fewer eyes."

"All the good points," Colton admitted. "Interesting," he repeated.

"Hey, you got to do what you got to do."

When Colton looked back again he saw a small snub-nose revolver pointed at him. "Is that the gun you killed Andy with?"

"I didn't kill Andy," the dealer said, taking several steps back. "But you are not a user, and I don't think you're a supplier either. You didn't come with any goods."

"Of course not," Colton said, laughing. "I don't know you from anyone, and I do know Andy is dead. So why would I bring anything here to a meeting with you?"

The guy sneered. "I don't like anything about this. You turn around and walk away, and you forget you ever saw me."

"If I turn around and walk away," Colton said calmly, staring him down, "you'll put a bullet in my back."

"Hell, no, but I might just put one between your eyes."

And, with that, Troy, who had slipped down the vehicles after seeing the gun, came up behind the man. And just as the gunman lifted his weapon and pointed it right at Colton's head, Troy took him down. With him on the ground, the handgun now tossed off to the side, Troy sitting on the guy's back, pinning his arms underneath him, Colton said, "Now we want to have a talk with you." He pulled out his temporary burner phone and contacted the commander. "You want to bring in the local police on this one?"

"I don't want to, no," he said. "But that is a citizen and not one of my men, so, yes, stay where you are and keep him there. I'll have the cops to you in just a few minutes."

"Will do," Colton said. "Keep in mind we don't know if the cops are clean."

There was a hesitation in the commander's voice as he said, "No, but I have to follow proper chains of authority, and I hope the people I'm calling understand that too.

Generally they don't have a drug problem here."

"Well, one has been uncovered. I can tell you, this one is a dealer, Andy was one of the dealers, and supplies have been coming through the base, so it will be a little hard to keep this hush-hush once this guy starts talking."

"If he starts talking."

Colton hung up and motioned at the man and said, "The cops are on the way."

The guy just laughed. "Like that'll make a fucking difference."

"Why is that?" Troy asked. Jerking him up to his feet, they secured his arms behind his back while Colton picked up the handgun. He studied it and nodded.

"Same model that put that bullet in Andy's head."

"I didn't do it," he said. "A few of those are around town. A guy was selling them about four years ago, and a bunch of us bought him out."

"Interesting," Colton said. "Who else would have one?"

At that, the dealer fell silent.

"And why is it we won't get any satisfaction out of the police?"

The look on the guy's face wasn't what Colton expected though. All the bravado was gone, and instead there was only fear. "I won't make it that far," he said. "I'll be taken out."

"Maybe you better start talking now then," Colton said. "Just to make sure you have a voice in what happens to your future."

"No," he said. "Once you take me into the station, I'm done for."

"Bad cops?" Troy asked from behind him.

The guy shook his head. "No, the goddamn cops here are too damn squeaky clean. You don't understand what it's like here, how many people don't own their own land. They just kind of live and borrow as needed."

"So why would you want to mess with a nice system like that?" Colton asked.

"Because they're all so innocent," he said. "We can move a lot of drugs through here."

"But through here is still through nowhere," Troy said. "You could have taken them to England and had a distribution network all through Europe."

"They get to England, but we can also hit all the Nordic countries and Russia. And we're coming down from Europe on the topside. It might take a little longer, but it's safer, with fewer roadblocks and fewer people in the know. You generally find the country folks are a little more naive when it comes to drugs. Hit any major port, and it's a damn puzzle to get stuff moving."

"And yet you say you'll be taken out if we get you to the police station."

"Once they figure out I'm being taken in, they'll assume I'll talk," he said.

"But who is *they*?" Colton asked.

"Those above me," he said, his shoulders sagging in defeat. "I'm already a dead man. You can bet somebody is watching us."

In the distance Colton could hear emergency vehicles coming. "That might be the cops now. Who killed Andy?"

"Not me." He looked up, smiled and said, "You still haven't figured it out, have you?"

"Not all of it," Colton said slowly. He needed more answers and desperately needed this guy to talk but wasn't sure what the magic was to get him to loosen up that tongue.

"That's because it's right in front of you," he said. "You

can't see it, and you're looking right at it."

"We know a couple pilots were involved, and they are in the custody of the military and have been since they were turned in," Troy said.

"Sure, but more will replace them."

"More military personnel?"

He shrugged. "It's a huge population to tap. A lot of users among the military—and a lot of dealers too. But the minute you get a network like that, you always get a couple who rise to the top."

"Right, the ones doing the drug running," Colton said.

His suspect nodded. "That's one way to look at it."

"And, of course, it has to be somebody at the Greenland base."

The man nodded again. "You're getting warmer."

Colton and Troy exchanged hard glances. "Who set up the pilot for this last run?"

"*Them*," he said with a hard emphasis.

"And that's because they were afraid George would do something and you'd lose the product?"

"Yeah," he said, "but more's coming in soon."

"Except for the bad weather."

"There's always bad weather here. It's one of the reasons the base isn't overrun with military resources, and that works really well."

"Does it move from one military branch to the other?" Troy asked.

"It's pretty easy to do that too. The military network is vast and is already in place."

"But it has to start somewhere. Any idea where it's coming from?"

He raised his gaze. "You got to be kidding me? The volume of drugs coming out of the US is massive."

"Sure," Colton said, "but how are they getting into the US?"

"That supply train has been moving steadily for decades. You'll never stop that one. It's a matter of getting it from one place to the next. The military provides a lovely global network."

Colton and Troy exchanged more glances. The guy was right. United States military bases were all over the world, and they did Joint Task Force operations with military units from multiple other countries as well. It was probably pretty simple to piggyback on that. "Did you guys have anything to do with blowing up the plane?"

The dealer shook his head. "I didn't know anything about that."

"Was it sabotage? Or was it the pilot?"

"I suspect both," he said. "If they didn't trust him, if he argued with them or told them what he might do, or maybe he sabotaged the plane on his own to get out of it. Or maybe it was a suicide mission. I don't know. He wouldn't be the first."

"Wouldn't be the first what?"

"To take his own life to get out of this hell. Once they get their claws into you, they learn everything they can about you and your family, and it's either follow their path or not."

As Colton went to ask something else, cop cars pulled into the parking lot toward them.

"Well, it's trouble now." The guy stared glumly. "I might yet get out of this," he said, "but I can't get out of it without blowing this wide open to get protection from the cops, then it hitting the news too."

"The media isn't likely to pick up your arrest, is it? Are

you wanted?"

He shook his head. "No, but gossips are everywhere. And the network on this island is unbelievable. Within five minutes of being booked into the police station, my head will be numbered."

With misgivings, Colton watched the cops load up their man. As one of the cops walked over to talk to him, Colton said, "I need an ID on who he is."

"That's Eric Strange," the cop said. "What's your business with him?" His suspicion was obvious, but as Colton and Troy explained what was going on, he relaxed and said, "I have instructions to move the information up the chain as it happens. I believe the commander will contact you as needed."

"I can only hope so," Colton said. He and Troy watched as the vehicle took off with Eric Strange in the back seat.

"Do you think Strange is right?" Troy asked.

"Unfortunately I think he probably is. He might not be marked right now, but tomorrow or the next day, yeah, it's possible. If this is as big of an operation or jumping point as he makes it sound, an awful lot is at risk."

"An awful lot is at risk, but it also means a pretty big deal if we can get it stopped," Troy said.

"What do you think he meant," Colton said, as they walked back toward the hospital, "about not seeing what's in front of us?"

"I'm afraid he means the base. Like whoever is masterminding this is somebody we've already spoken to."

"*Great.* The good news is," Colton said, "the shipment wasn't full of drugs, so there's no point in going through a recovery operation. And another plane is coming in soon with more."

"Right," Troy said. "Something else we'll have to brief the commander on."

"Let's collect Kate and head back," Colton said. "She'll need food, and it's been a long day already."

"Productive in many ways though," Troy said. "One dead man, one captured man, and George is awake."

As they wandered back up toward his room, they could hear George and Kate inside. When they walked in, she looked up, and a big smile crossed her face. Colton felt his heart warm in response. He held out his hand, and she slipped under his arm and gave him a big hug. "There you are," she exclaimed. "I was starting to wonder if you were okay."

"Not to worry," he said. "It's all good." He looked over at George and smiled. "You're looking better than the last time I saw you," he said with a little emotion in his voice.

George reached out a bandaged hand and said, "I want to thank you for saving my life."

"I'm not exactly sure what happened," Colton said. "So I'm not sure if you're responsible for the plane being ditched or not."

"I was partly responsible," George said. "The end result was not at all what I had planned, so I'm not sure if it was my actions that did it or not, but I definitely didn't want to bring that plane into the base."

"If it makes you feel any better," Colton said, "we just spoke to one of the men involved in this mess, and he said your plane didn't have any drugs on it. It was a test to see if you were trustworthy."

"I guess I failed that then, didn't I?"

"Exactly," Colton said with a smile. "On the other hand, I'm sure the military is happy to hear that."

"They aren't, however, happy about something else," Troy said, leaning against the doorway. "Apparently the base is being used as a jumping off point for distribution on the northern network."

"Crap," George said. "That's really disturbing."

"The fact that we even know this much," Colton said, "will help us track it down."

"But the bad weather will stop the next plane coming in, won't it?"

"Yes, but ..." Troy said, turning to look at Colton. "Did he actually say it was coming into the base?"

Colton thought about it for a long moment, then shook his head. "You know something? I don't think he did."

He looked over at George. "Sorry about the toes."

"Hey, I'll trade my toes and a couple fingers for my life any day. Maybe it's time to take an early retirement and go spend time with the boys who I'm fighting so hard to get back home to." He looked over at Kate. "Kate here can keep up the runs."

"Hey, you know me," Kate said. "I was wondering about changing up my schedule too."

Colton looked at her in surprise.

She shrugged. "I wouldn't mind more time at home," she confessed. "Especially once the Ned issue is handled."

"Do you have enough seniority to change your routes?" he asked. "Or do you want to go private?"

"Both are things I'll consider over the next few weeks and months," she said. Looking back at George, she smiled. "The bottom line is to get you healthy."

"And keep you safe," Colton said, as he stepped out and looked at the doorway. "When did the guards leave?"

George's eyebrows rose. "I didn't see any guards today."

162

The three exchanged hard glances. Troy said, "Wait here. I'll go find out." Then he disappeared down the hallway.

"You didn't mention anything about guards," George said to Kate.

"I forgot all about them," she exclaimed. "After what happened yesterday, a security detail was assigned. We waited here for them to arrive. They took up their posts outside your room, and we headed back to the base."

"So, who pulled them off the guard duty detail?" Colton said slowly. He grabbed his phone and dialed the commander. When he answered, Colton said, "We're checking in on George, but the security detail is gone."

"It shouldn't be. They were supposed to be standing on a twenty-four-hour watch." The commander's voice rose in anger. "I'll get back to you."

Colton pocketed his phone. "Heads will roll." His voice was cheerful though because he liked to see people follow orders, and to see something like this happen meant that either somebody had changed the orders or somebody was trying to get out of following orders. In either case, somebody was about to get their ass handed to them. He said, "I guess that means we'll sit here and wait until we get this sorted out again."

George shook his head. "Go on. I'm fine."

"No, you're not," Kate said, walking over to the bedside chair and sitting down. "You weren't fine yesterday, and you won't be fine today, should someone come in here, intending harm."

"It's almost dinnertime already," he said. "I don't know how long you guys have been here, but you look exhausted and cold."

"I don't know about you," Kate said, motioning at him in the bed, "but I'm always cold now."

He nodded. "Yeah, I've got a few more blankets than a person should need. But I'm hoping that'll ease up over time."

"It will," she said. "Over time."

They stayed and visited with casual small talk until Troy came back. "They were released early this morning."

"Released or replaced?"

"The nursing staff thought they were supposed to be replaced, but nobody else showed up."

"The commander is on it now too," Colton said. Just then his phone rang.

"Stay where you are," the commander said, "I have two more men coming."

"Apparently they were released this morning," Colton said.

"They were to be replaced, but the order didn't go through as issued. Don't worry. I'll find out why." And, from the tone of his voice, Colton realized he was beyond furious.

"Understood." Colton hung up and said, "We're to wait until the new detail arrives."

George shrugged. "An awful lot of fuss over nothing."

"Not nothing," Kate said. "Keeping you safe is the difference between having a witness and evidence to the blackmail and not. If we want to stop this, we have to stop it, not just slow it down."

George nodded. "I was kind of hoping I could go home to my family and put this behind me."

"You'll never put it behind you," Colton said, "until it's over. And you're at risk until it is."

CHAPTER 13

K ATE HATED TO think Colton was serious, but it was pretty obvious he was. She was tired and hungry and was more than ready for an early night again. She couldn't believe just how exhausting this day had been, but the shock of finding that poor dead man and then waiting for the cops and walking around the houses to question the locals and all had made for a very long and tiring day. Not to mention her long and emotionally taxing reunion with George. Her energy reserves were already thin, and now they had been maxed out completely. It was a relief to see Colton and Troy step out into the hallway to greet two new soldiers. And then Colton looked at her and said, "We should get going now."

She smiled and, leaning over, gave George a kiss on the cheek and said, "You stay safe." She walked out to meet Colton and wrapped an arm around his waist, his arm instinctively coming around her shoulder. "So how are we getting back to the base?"

"Parsons is coming to get us again," Troy said.

She smiled, then nodded and said, "Perfect." Outside, they waited for a vehicle to come. Finally a military vehicle did pull up. It was Parsons.

"Sorry," he said, "I didn't get the orders until I was back at base again."

"It's been a long day for everyone," Kate said, sliding

into the front seat, while Troy and Colton took the back. By now darkness was settling in, but it wasn't the darkness of night; it was the storm and the cloud cover taking over. She looked up and groaned. "It looks like a crappy day weather-wise too."

"It is a crappy day," Parsons said. And it probably was for him because of the news and whatever the commander had told him or possibly even reamed him out about. He didn't look terribly impressed either. As they drove back to the base, Kate could hear the men in the back seat talking. She twisted a couple times, but their voices were low as they compared notes and showed each other texts. She didn't understand what was going on, and she knew Parsons himself was curious too. Finally she looked around to face forward again and realized they'd taken a different route this time. "Where are we?"

Parsons yawned. "It's faster this way," he said, "particularly if the weather is getting bad."

She settled back and said, "I'm so damn tired."

"Did you eat?" Parsons asked. "I have a flask of coffee down there, if you want."

She was tempted, and then she shook her head. "No, it's all right. I'll just close my eyes. Wake me up when we get there."

He gave a bark of laughter. "No problem. I can do that."

She dozed a little. Finally she looked up to see headlights coming toward them. "Are we almost there?"

"We are," Parsons said.

She looked out to see an almost empty wasteland of a road. "It's very different country here."

"Very," he said.

Just then a vehicle came up behind them and another

one ahead. Kate looked from one vehicle to the other, and then checked on the guys to see that they were both aware. She frowned at Colton, but he lifted a finger to his lips. She sagged back, but her nerves were shot as she realized something was going on that she didn't understand. She could tell from Parsons' reactions as he looked from window to window that he wasn't happy either.

"A lot of traffic," she murmured.

"Too much," he said. "It's unusual."

Just then, the vehicle ahead hit its brakes and started to slow down.

"What's up ahead?" she asked Parsons. "Is that the base?" The ugly weather was dark enough with clouds churning all around them that it was hard to see much.

"It could be an obstruction on the road," he said. As they went to drive past the vehicle, it turned at an angle, blocking the road. "It happens when there's a road slide or some other problem. There could be an accident I don't know about or something." He pulled off to the side and said, "Stay here."

He hopped out and went to talk to the men in the truck up ahead, around to the driver's side and then carried on around to the front of the engine, the vehicle now blocking view of Parsons.

Troy and Colton both said, "We want you to stay inside." They opened the doors and slipped out. And then she saw the guns.

And the gunmen were US military personnel, all in fatigues.

Somebody was coming up behind Colton, holding a handgun against him. And the same for Troy. And she realized that whether Parsons was a part of it or not, this was a trap. And they were well and truly caught. She slipped out of the vehicle, wondering if she should head cross-country. She looked over at Colton, and he yelled, "Run."

Swearing, she raced ahead to the front vehicle, looking for any place to hide and to get away from here. Just when she was ready to bolt, she heard gunfire. She was out of sight of both Troy and Colton and decided on a more dangerous move than she'd expected. She threw herself under the big rig in front of them.

And, from here, she checked out where all the legs were. Two in front and four on the left. So three men were nearby, and then one collapsed to the ground. It was Parsons. He held his shoulder, which oozed blood, but he was facing away from her. She didn't know if she could help him or not, and yelling came from the two men still standing.

Then Colton and Troy were brought over, which meant a total of six men that she could see, plus Parsons on the ground. She was completely outnumbered, and it wouldn't take long for somebody to figure out she'd either taken off cross-country, or she'd hidden somewhere. And the chances and options to hide were slim. She was only minutes away from being found.

But, as long as all the men were on one side of the vehicle, she could head somewhere else. She rolled out to the other side and headed back to the military jeep which Parsons had been driving. She climbed into the open passenger door, slipped over to the driver's seat, then turned on the engine.

Instead of backing up and turning around, she yanked the wheels hard and drove off-road until she'd circled around, then drove back onto the pavement. And she hit the gas as hard as she could. Shots were fired in her direction, but nothing hit the vehicle. She didn't know where she was going or how far, but she needed to get the hell away.

Another vehicle came up in front of her, but she had no way of knowing if it held good guys or bad guys, and she didn't dare take a chance of choosing wrong, so she slowed. When they pulled out and crossed the road in front of her, she realized exactly who they were. The men were out and holding guns on her within seconds. She lifted her hands slowly, and they ordered her from the vehicle. She stepped out and saw they were from the base too. At gunpoint she was marched back up the road a good mile to where she'd left the men.

When Colton saw her, the muscle at the corner of his jaw started twitching. She ran to him, and he wrapped his arms around her and held her close.

"Isn't that cute," one of the men said.

"Not really," Colton growled. "What the hell is this all about?"

"Drugs of course."

"So you're part of this?"

Troy asked, "How the hell can you do that? You're supposed to be serving your country."

"What the hell has my country done for me?" he said. "Good thing we had our last truck coming up behind us. He was supposed to get in early, but he didn't make it."

So now there were even more men to deal with. She looked over at Troy to see he had a handgun hidden at his back. Had he brought it with him? Or taken it off someone? Troy stepped slightly closer to her, gave her a hug and whispered, "When things blow, get under the truck."

And, with that, he stepped forward, grabbed the gun arm of the man closest to him, then turned it and shot the man who'd been speaking. Kate dropped to the ground and rolled under the truck as chaos broke loose. Shots were fired in all directions. She slipped up to where Parsons lay very still and took his revolver from his holster and waited for things to calm down.

As she peered out, she could see two men now holding their guns on Troy. She rose up on her elbows and fired, taking one man out with a headshot. Troy grabbed the other, knocked him to the ground and subdued him. Kate wasn't sure if that was everybody, but Colton dropped to his knees to find her. "Is it safe to come out now?"

He helped her roll out from underneath and back onto her feet. He looked at the gun, and she nodded.

"I got it off Parsons." Parsons was on the ground, softly moaning.

"We've got a lot of men down now," Colton said, already dialing his phone.

Kate walked over to Troy. "Are you okay?"

He nodded grimly. "A couple of burns but nothing major. It's Colton who's been shot."

She spun around to look at him. Colton just shrugged, and she could see blood welling up on his leg. She ran back to the truck, looking for a first-aid kit. Not finding any, she went to the guy she'd shot in the head and ripped his T-shirt off. With Troy's help, they cut off a big strip. While Colton was still talking to the commander, she bound up his leg.

When she was done, he looked down and smiled. "It wasn't that bad, you know?"

"You're tracking blood everywhere," Kate said, as if cleanliness were the most important thing here. Then she laughed and sat back on her haunches. Looking up at him, she said, "You know what? We're damn lucky to have survived this."

"Damn lucky," Troy said. "And I owe you my life."

She shook her head. "I think we're all past that at this point. It seems like we've done nothing but save each other."

She looked down at Parsons and said, "How bad is he?"

"Not," Troy said. "But the commander is sending in the troops."

At that, Parsons managed to sit up. "Wow," he said. "Talk about an ambush."

She nodded. "Do I need to work on your shoulder?"

"No," he said. "I'll just sit here and wait until the rescue comes." He smiled up at her. "Can I get my gun back please?"

She handed it to him without a thought. Immediately he reached up and fired a shot. She took the bullet in her shoulder and stared at him in shock. The gun went off a second time, but she was already on her way to the ground when the burn slashed into the same damn shoulder.

COLTON BOLTED TOWARD Parsons, only to be facing the handgun.

Parsons smiled up at him. "Fooled you, huh?"

Colton just glared at him, the muscle in his jaw working. It was sure death to take a step forward. But Kate was lying beside him unconscious, and he didn't know how badly hurt she was.

"I didn't kill her," Parsons said, "if that means anything to you."

"Not much," Colton said, his voice deadly soft.

"Of course not. You're one of those big macho guys. Got to do everything right."

"Not necessarily," Colton said. "But we're also in a relationship, and I really don't appreciate you shooting her."

"And I really don't appreciate you guys getting in my face," Parsons said.

"Is this all your deal?" Troy asked, taking a step forward.

"One more step," Parsons said, "and I'll blow your friend's brains out."

Troy stopped moving. But even Colton could feel the assessment in his hard gaze.

"How do you plan to get out of this now?" Colton asked.

"I need a moment to figure that out," Parsons said. "Somehow you guys managed to wipe everybody out. I mean, I've seen a lot of guys who were damn good, but I wasn't expecting this. You guys are a cut above." He looked at the men on the ground around him. "Like, what the hell?"

"If you'd stayed quiet," Troy said at Colton's side, "nobody would have known."

"You don't know anything now. But it wouldn't take long I'm sure before it would come out."

"All you had to do though was stay quiet. Pack up on leave and never bother coming back," Colton said persuasively. "You can still do that."

"You think I'll get off Greenland safely?"

"Do you really think, after all this, you'll still salvage this somehow?"

"If I kill you three," he said, "then nobody will know."

"The commander has already been brought in on this," Colton said.

Parsons stared at him. "You've already reported in?"

"I could show you my phone to see it for yourself. Some of it was telephone, and some of it was text."

At that, Parsons started swearing. "Goddammit. He could have another half dozen vehicles on the way."

"If we don't check in soon, he certainly will." Colton glanced around. "Exactly where are we anyway?"

"It's a back way to the base," Parsons said. "But it's not exactly the easiest way to go."

"So why did you go this way?"

"Because they do a lot of practice out here, and I knew some of the guys could come and give me a hand without being noticed."

"So you arranged this lovely little ambush?"

"If that's what you want to call it, yes. Rescue is the other answer."

Troy just shook his head.

Colton agreed because none of it made any sense. "I still don't understand why you blew your cover. You were set up to walk away as an injured good guy. With that injury you might very well have just gotten a discharge and stepped out."

"Maybe," he said. "But I figured, with you guys in the middle of this headache, and George still alive, there wasn't any way to walk away free and clear."

"Are you the one who attacked George?"

Parsons waved his gun at him. "Just shut the fuck up right now," he said. "I have to think."

Colton went quiet, but he watched the sweat on the man's face. Not only was the pain making it hard for Parsons to think clearly, but he was in a pickle.

"The easiest thing would be to say you were pressured into doing this," Colton said in a conversational tone.

The gun was immediately pointed at him again.

"I said shut the hell up," Parsons snapped. Using the

truck, he slowly stood, keeping the gun leveled on Colton and Troy. When Troy stepped forward, Parsons smiled and said, "I don't really care if I kill both of you or not, but you know for sure your buddy will be dead because I can't miss at this range."

Colton said, "But you're not likely to kill both of us. And that'll still leave you with one death on your record. At the moment I don't see any on yours. These guys," he said, waving his arm, "are all on us."

"And I'm still figuring out how you did that," Parsons said. "None of it makes any sense."

"Makes more sense than you think," Troy said cheerfully. "It's kind of what we do."

"Hell, I'm military," Parsons said. "What the hell are you guys?"

"Navy SEALs," Colton said, his voice hard and dry. "If you got your fat ass off the ground and into the water, you might have learned a little more."

"Well, that just means you're sea, air and land. I'm just land, but I should still be better than you."

At that Colton's eyebrows shot up. "Not sure how you figured that," he said, "but whatever."

"The *whatevers* in life count," Parsons said, but it was obvious the pain and maybe the blood loss was starting to get to him. "I can't handle two of you, so I'll have to kill one. The other one will drive me out of here."

"Maybe," Troy said. "What will you do about her?"

"I'll shoot her," he said.

"Wow," Colton said. "So you've got absolutely no problem shooting a defenseless unconscious woman on the ground. That's like shooting one of us in the back. Absolutely no honor in that."

"Honor? There is no honor in this job. I've been trying to get off this goddamn base for four years, and I haven't been able to. At first I thought, if I was good as gold, I'd get a transfer. Instead, they just kept me on because I was so damn good at my job. At some point my dissatisfaction turned to hatred. And that hatred turned to revenge and trying to find any way I could to screw this place. When I finally figured it out and hooked up with the drug-running, life became interesting. I'm not even too bothered about leaving now, except for the fact that you busted my position here wide open. Who the hell needs that?"

"That won't stop now, no matter what you do to us," Troy said. "The commander is already running a full investigation. Plus we already know the next plane that comes in will have the real drugs. The one George flew in with Kate was supposed to have drugs, but they were running it as a test, and it literally was just cargo."

"So I heard. Figures I wouldn't hear about it until afterward. All I could think about was all that money sitting in the Arctic Ocean."

"You can always try to recoup some of it," Colton said cheerfully. "But I highly doubt I would trust anything anybody says in your outfit."

"That's the problem," Parsons said. "I can't trust anyone. I can't trust the people who told me it was full of drugs, and I can't trust you guys telling me it was a trick. The trouble is, I can see them doing the trick thing to test out members in the chain to see if we're loyal."

"If you're making money on this," Colton said, "then that's a smart way to be. Nobody is loyal long-term. They're only loyal as long as it benefits them."

"By the way, did you kill Andy?" Troy asked, studying

Parsons like he was a bug he'd never seen before.

"Forget about Andy," Parsons said.

"Why is that?"

"Andy already botched his situation at the base, and getting him out of there without getting court-martialed was a trick, but I managed it. I figured he could be useful from town, but then he stopped being useful."

"Wow," Colton said. "And what about the plane? Did you guys sabotage it?"

"No, it was all part of the trick to keep George honest. But instead he ditched the plane."

"I'm not so sure about that," Colton said, "because the engine did blow up."

"I wondered about that too. It's possible that, when the bosses realized George wouldn't do what they told him, they blew it up to get rid of him anyway. I don't know. They don't tell me anything."

"How will we deal with them?"

"You won't," Parsons said. "Some are at Coronado base. Some are on the German base. They're all over the place. They infiltrate even the big military groups. Once you're in, you're caught, and you follow orders."

"Like ordering you to take others out, like Andy."

"Didn't have a choice with Andy. And look at the guys you've just taken out now." Parsons's gaze cast around to the dead men on the ground, and he shook his head. "A bloody massacre."

"They pulled guns on us," Troy said softly.

Colton just gave Parsons a fat grin. "And you do see the relevance of what you're holding on us now, right?"

"It's not as if you guys will stop me," Parsons said, "at this distance nobody could miss."

"Sorry to say," Colton said, "we're willing to take our chances."

Parsons stared at that. "You're willing to take certain death for one of you in order to make sure you stop me?"

"For what you did to Kate, absolutely," Colton said.

"And what you did to Andy and George and possibly a half-dozen others," Troy said.

"How is that sensible? Why don't you just decide between you which guy will die, and the other one get in the damn vehicle and drive me back into town. I need medical attention."

"You'll take the gun into the hospital and force them to treat you too?"

"Sure," he said and smiled. "Actually, you know something? I think we'll put her inside the vehicle too. We'll keep her as collateral, to make sure you behave. And, if you don't, I'll blow you all apart."

"You won't get far," Colton said.

"You keep giving me that bullshit," Parsons said, looking around at the vehicles, "but I don't want one of these big rigs."

"What do you want?" Troy asked helpfully.

"I want the one she took in the first place."

"I can go get it," Troy said.

"And take off on me?" Parsons said derisively. "I wasn't born yesterday."

"No, but you have her and Colton captive," Troy said. "Of course I'll come back."

"I don't know. I don't feel like I can trust you."

"I'll do anything to stop you from shooting these two," Troy said quietly. "Hasn't there been enough death already?"

"Go get it and bring it back because you can bet that, if

you don't, I'll have people waiting for you at the other end."

"Why don't you bring some people in here to grab your guys so they're all taken care of?"

"No, we'll figure out how to blame this all on you."

Just then the wind picked up, and Colton's hair whipped back tight around his head. He brushed it back, turning his face into the wind. He looked over at Troy, and they could see how black and dark the clouds were. He yelled over the wind, "We have to do something soon, or we won't be going anywhere." He could see the vehicles rocking in the wind. "Come on. We have to get you somewhere to get treatment."

Parsons took several deep breaths. "It's not that easy," he said.

"It's not that hard."

Troy made a decision and said, "I'll go get the jeep," and he took off at a run. From his position, Parsons couldn't even move to stop him. He just held the gun on Colton.

"You're not going anywhere," he said.

"What will you do if he takes off?"

"I don't know," he said, but his breath was gaspy and choppy. "It's not how I wanted to go out."

"Then don't make this a case of going out," Colton said. "You can do this. Let me give you some help. You don't have to die from this."

"If I don't get help soon though, I will. I don't have any choice. I'm losing too much blood."

Colton studied the man, seeing the pale waxy look to his skin, the sweat on his forehead and the odd fevered look to his eyes. "How badly are you hurt?"

"Bad enough," he said, then he started to swear. "God damn it, this is not what I wanted."

"Then let me help you," Colton snapped. "Even if you do a few years, you'll still be alive."

"It won't be a few years, and, just like Andy, I'll be taken out. And the dealer you sent off to jail today? He'll get taken out too."

"If he hasn't already," Colton said with a nod. "That's what he said would happen."

"Exactly, and it'll happen to me too."

"I doubt it," Colton said. "Let me help you. We'll get you back to the base, and the doctors can help you."

"No," he said. "Not the base. They'll shoot me for sure."

"Tell us who else is involved in the drugs."

"I don't know—somebody, but I don't know who."

"Above you?"

Parsons nodded. "Yeah, definitely above me."

"No idea, no hints?"

"None," he said, and slowly he sagged to the ground. Colton took the gun from his hand, then tucked it into the back of his jeans and said, "Damn it, man, you don't have to die from this."

"I think it's too late," Parsons whispered.

Colton ripped Parsons's shirt apart and studied his shoulder. He grabbed more of the T-shirt that had been used to tie up his leg. It was sitting on the ground, already dirty and getting rained on, but it was something. He folded it with the cleanest side out, then pressed it against the shoulder and said, "Here. Hold this." And, while Parsons held it tight, Colton checked Parsons's vitals and said, "Were you shot anywhere else?"

"No, but I think it must have nicked something major."

Colton stepped back and walked to where Kate lay and checked her shoulder.

In her case both bullet holes were generally superficial wounds, so it must have been the shock that dropped her. She opened her eyes slowly and looked up at him. "Did you stop him?"

"I did," he said. He helped her into a sitting position. "You took two hits, but one of them was more of a burn."

"It just seemed like a huge stab wound," she said. "I didn't know how bad it was, then everything went blank."

"Yeah, that second shot put you down like a ton of bricks."

"That's a good description," she said, "because that's how I feel." He helped her back to where Parsons sat, then helped her inside a vehicle, out of the rain that was starting to pick up.

"Let's get you inside, both of you." He could hear a vehicle coming toward them.

Parsons smiled. "I guess your buddy meant it."

"Yeah, he meant it," Colton said. "He also knew I'd have no trouble taking you out."

"Damn," Parsons said. "I was only fooling myself, wasn't I?"

"Yeah," Colton said, "you were."

The vehicle pulled up and parked beside them. Troy hopped out, and, seeing Kate sitting on the driver's side, helped her to the other vehicle. He buckled her in, then came back, picked up Parsons and loaded him in the back. Then Colton and Troy checked on all the men on the ground. But nobody was left alive, so they hopped in the military jeep, with Troy driving and Colton in the back to keep an eye on Parsons. Troy turned around and headed back toward town.

"You could keep going the other way," Parsons said. "It

would be faster."

"Is it though? What's the road like?" Troy asked, turning to look at him.

"It's not bad. You've got about another fifteen miles to go. It would be faster. By the time you head back to town in this storm, you won't get back to the base."

"I'm not sure I care to go back to the base anyway," Troy said. "We need to pick up these men."

"Why don't we do that?" Colton asked. "Let's load them up into the back of the bigger truck, and we'll drive them into the base." So, with that, Troy turned around, and he and Colton carefully loaded up all the men into the back of the first truck. Then Colton returned to the jeep and looked at Kate. "Are you okay to stay there while Troy drives?"

She nodded slowly. "Yeah," she said. "As long as we're getting out of this storm." By now the thunder was crackling and the lightning flashing, and the wind was terrible. Her words were picked up and swept away every time she opened her mouth. Colton nodded, raced back to the big truck, started it up and drove off. Through the rearview mirror, he could see them following him, so he stepped on the gas and kept going.

CHAPTER 14

Talk about feeling like shit. Kate turned to look at Parsons, who was leaning on the back seat, his eyes closed. "Why the hell did you have to shoot me not once but twice?" she growled.

"Sorry," he said, "at least I shot high."

"Yeah, but you also could have killed me," she said. "Instead, my shoulder is killing me."

"I probably won't make it through the storm anyway," he muttered. "So, whatever."

She had to admit that was a hell of an argument. She looked over at Troy. "The storm is really picking up, isn't it?"

He nodded grimly. "There's a reason why we were all supposed to stay on base."

"Or in town," she said.

"True enough." Just then a heavy blast of wind hit the jeep sideways. It didn't dislodge it off the road, but it buffeted them heavily.

"Should we have gone in the big truck too?" Kate cried out.

"If it gets too bad," Troy said, "we'll move to Colton's truck."

"Right," Kate said. They were staying close behind where at least they could still see the faint glow of the rear taillights. But that was about it. It was all shadows with no sign of the road anywhere. "I hope his visibility is better than ours."

"I doubt it," Troy said. "It's all I can do to see him. What's he following?"

She stayed silent at that. "So how will we know if we're even still on the road?"

"We are," Troy said, pointing to the edges of the shoulder. "I'm keeping an eye on that too."

"It's just nasty out here. I've seen a lot of storms, but not like this."

"The storms they get up here," Parsons said faintly from the back seat, "they're brutal."

"So it's a good night for murder and mayhem then, isn't it?" she snapped.

He didn't say anything. She turned. "Who above you is involved?"

"Don't know."

"What about those below you?"

"Don't know," he said. "Andy and Strange were the ones who handled that."

"Strange is in custody," Kate said, "so hopefully the cops can get answers from him. But we're heading into the base, which means going to whoever is still controlling this. So any answers you have that will help keep us alive would be appreciated."

"It won't keep me alive," Parsons said.

"So, if it won't do you any good, you don't want to help anybody else?" Kate asked. She waited a moment and then prodded him again. "Don't you have any siblings? Don't you want people to know you lived a life of honor instead of shame?"

He just glared at her.

She nodded. "Either you can help or you can go down as a traitor. What do you want your family to hear?"

"Of course I don't want them to know about this shit," he said. "They were never supposed to hear about it."

"And yet," she said, "that's not what'll happen. You'll go down as part of a drug-running group the military cleaned out. I have no idea what they'll do for a pension if you have a wife," she said. "I imagine you'll be dishonorably discharged, with no benefits, but I don't know."

"I don't know either," Parsons said. "When you get involved in shit like this, you don't think about the consequences on that end. And, to a certain extent, I still don't. I don't have a wife. I don't have any kids, and my mother is gone. There's my father and my brother, and I would just as soon they didn't know about this, but I don't know who it is working above me."

"So how did it work?" Kate asked. "The drugs come in, so who loads them onto the vehicles?"

"The dead guys," Parsons said faintly.

"And you?"

"I check the manifests and keep the product moving," he said.

"How do you know somebody is above you?"

"Because the planes have to come in and be approved, and all the cargo has to be moved. People have to sign that."

"What does it come in as?"

"Medical supplies usually," he said. "Or basic supplies for the base."

Kate nodded and sat back, wondering. "Do you think the commander is involved?"

"No," he said. "The commander has always been good

to me. And I'm sorry he'll find out about this."

"Not as sorry as he'll be," she muttered. "He put his trust in you, and look how you repaid him."

"Guilt really doesn't matter much now," Parsons said, gasping.

"But it makes me feel better," she snapped. "All of this is just bullshit. I almost died several times now because of it, and all I was doing was bringing a plane load of supplies into the base."

"You delivered drugs before too," he said with a sneer. "You get a manifest, and, as far as you're concerned, all of the cargo has been loaded up, and you fly it. You don't know what's being flown. There is no doubt drugs have made it onto your loads many times."

"Great," she said in a whisper. "That's not what I want to hear."

"No, maybe not," he said. "But again somebody has to be signing this paperwork."

"What about in purchasing?"

"Maybe," he said, "but somebody higher up has to okay the orders."

"That takes us back to the commander," she said. "Aren't you his right-hand man?"

"Yep," he said, "and I did sign a lot of the paperwork. But a lot of the stuff I didn't."

"So you signed on his behalf?"

He nodded. "I knew that wouldn't last too long either. Just think about it. Not everybody will believe that the commander was bringing in forty pallets of toilet paper."

"Actually pallets of toilet paper make a lot of sense," she said.

"If one of those pallets is drugs, nobody checks."

"Shit," Troy said from the driver's side. "I can see that. For a base like this, you need a ton of supplies."

"And easy enough to hide drugs in the shipments to move as needed," he said. "It just gets moved into the back of another truck, so we had men at every level."

"Great," she said. "That doesn't sound good."

"It doesn't matter. It happens in every big organization. Company theft or moving things through the company is a common problem."

"Never where I worked," she said. "Or no one I ever worked with anyway."

"Which is why you wouldn't have been included," Parsons said, "but, trust me, every corporation has a group like that."

Troy nodded. "Unfortunately he's right."

Kate stared. "That's pretty sad."

"It's realistic," Troy said shortly. Another heavy gust of wind slammed into the jeep, jolting her sideways. "Damn," she said, "I feel like we won't make it to the base."

"We'll have to sit in the vehicles, if that's the case," Troy said.

She looked ahead and could see Colton still driving steadily. "I guess as long as he's moving forward, we are too."

"Yep."

She looked back at Parsons. "How much farther?"

"Shouldn't be too much longer," he said. "It's hard to say though."

Then Troy pointed and said, "Look."

Up ahead through the heavy storm were lights. "Is that the base?"

Parsons nodded.

COLTON HATED TO admit it, but he was damned relieved to see the base. A part of him had been worried Parsons had sent him into another ambush. But as he entered and opened his window to the man at the gate, he explained who he was and what he was doing. He said, "Call the commander and have him meet us down here too."

With that, the gate opened, and he drove through, and he could see Troy had been stopped as well, but he was eventually let through too. The gates closed heavily behind them. There shouldn't be anybody else coming and going, but somebody needed to stand watch just in case.

Colton drove up to the warehouse on the left. He wasn't sure where the hell to go, but this one had a door partially open, and he figured he could get inside and unload their cargo. Although he might have been better off going into town and taking them right to the hospital and to the morgue. As he drove in, his phone went off. He answered it. "Commander, I'm just pulling into a warehouse. I've got eight men dead in the back."

"Jesus Christ! I'm on my way," he said. "What the hell is this about Parsons?"

"You better come down here, sir. It's pretty bad."

As Colton pocketed his phone, he hopped out and opened up the big warehouse door farther so he could get in under it. Hanging onto the vehicle every step of the way in order to not get thrown sideways, he hopped back into the truck and drove it in. Immediately the heavy sound of the wind stopped, muffled by the structure. He pulled over to one side so Troy could pull up beside him. As soon as he shut off the engine, he opened the truck door, hopped down and opened the door for Kate. He looked at her, seeing the fatigue and the exhaustion in her face. "How you holding up?"

"I'm okay," she said. "But I guess we missed another meal, didn't we?"

He just grinned and helped her out. Just then half-a-dozen men swarmed into the warehouse. At the orders to halt and raise their hands, he lifted his. Kate lifted hers as much as she could, but her shoulder was killing her.

The commander stepped forward. "Colton?"

"Here, sir," he said. He lowered his hands and moved Kate forward. "She has been shot twice, compliments of Parsons."

The commander's eyebrows shot up. "Jesus. Where is he?"

Troy stepped forward. "He's in the back of this vehicle, sir."

The commander strode forward, fury, frustration and maybe a little grief on his face as he opened the door, and there was Parsons, lying flat out now. The commander checked for a pulse.

Parsons whispered, "Sorry, sir."

"Damn it, man."

"Got in over my head, sir. Couldn't see my way out. It'd be nice if you wouldn't tell my father and brother." He looked up the commander and said, "Yeah, I messed up big time." And, with that, he closed his eyes, and, in front of everybody present, he took his last breath and expired. After that, it was chaos.

Colton opened up the back of the big truck and brought the commander around to take a look. When he saw the dead men were from his own base, and Colton told him about the ambush, the commander swore up and down. But he issued orders quickly. As the men started removing the bodies from the back of the truck, Colton pulled the commander aside and told him that Parsons had said this involved US bases all over the world. But here, at Thule, somebody was upwind of Parsons, but he said he didn't know who.

The commander glared at Colton, shaking his head, his mouth a grim taut line.

"He did clear you, sir," he said, a tiny grin at the corner of his mouth. He knew he was insulting the commander, but at least he would also know he'd been cleared.

"This is unbelievable. So he was signing my signature to smuggle drugs into *my* base?"

Troy stepped up beside him. "Yes, sir," and he related the last little bit that Parsons had shared. "He said he really didn't know who it was, but he did mention medical supplies."

At that, the commander's jaw worked. "Then I guess we better deal with the corpses first. Hell, I don't even know if we have room for them all." He headed out after the last one was taken away, and all headed to the sick bay.

Although nobody was technically on duty, two doctors raced toward him. When they saw the line of dead soldiers, their faces showed anger and grief.

"What happened?" one of them snapped.

"Good question," said the commander, his voice powerful and brooking no argument. "I'd like to see all the medical personnel who are here, including the nurses, please."

It took about ten minutes before there was a full assembly.

The commander looked them over. "We highly suspect at least one of you has been helping this group of dead men run a drug operation through this base. I don't have time to deal with finding out which one of you it is, so step forward now, and it'll go slightly easier on you. Make me do a full investigation, and I'll make sure all of you, including your families, pay for this," he roared.

There was dead silence, as everybody processed his words.

Colton stepped forward and said, "We understand a ton of medical supplies have been ordered, but what's been coming also are drugs. Somebody has been signing those forms."

Kate was at his side, and she addressed the doctor she had seen earlier. "Please tell me that it wasn't you."

He looked at her in surprise. "Why do you care?"

"Because Parsons shot me, *twice*," she said bitterly. "And I came here to get medical treatment. The three of us are the only ones who got shot and survived today," she said. "Another man in town was murdered, and a second is likely to be taken out, even though he's in prison. Parsons didn't make it, and, as you can see from the rest gathered here, nobody else made it either. I don't understand how anybody in the profession of saving lives could be dealing in drugs that are killing people."

Several of the doctors said, "I didn't have anything to do with it."

However, Colton watched Kate as she studied the doctor she'd seen, her gaze steady, as if she knew something he didn't. Casually Colton walked over and around, behind the doctors, as if going to the cabinet. And, just as he went past, he took a look at the doctor whose hand was in his pocket. Something was there. Colton pulled out the handgun he'd taken off Parsons and held it against the doctor's ribs. "Pull your hand out gently," he ordered. "Now."

He pulled his hand out, and, sure enough, he had a handgun. "Of course I needed the handgun," the doctor snapped. "You just brought a mess of dead men into my medical clinic. I have to be prepared for anything."

"I wonder if that's what you were protecting or if you were just waiting for an opportunity to get out of this. Even maybe shoot your way out," Kate said quietly.

He continued to glare at her.

The commander addressed him now. "Brody?"

Brody and the commander glared at each other. And then the commander's shoulders sagged. "Jesus, Brody. Why?"

Brody shrugged. "I needed the money."

"But why?" the commander asked, lifting his shoulders. It was obvious from the interplay that they were friends and that this was a betrayal the commander hadn't seen coming.

"Cheryl left me," he said. "She took everything. The bank accounts, the house, the kids, the vehicles, literally everything. And since I'm the one with the paycheck, I'll get stuck paying alimony to boot. The last time you told me to take a leave," he said, "I didn't have anywhere to go. I ended up staying in town and was approached by this group. They offered me a path to retirement that she couldn't touch and enough spending money so I could go someplace on my days off without losing everything."

"Instead you'll lose it all anyway," Kate said.

"Maybe so, but I want to make sure she doesn't get more."

"What about your kids?" Kate asked.

As if understanding something more was going on, Colton watched the interplay suspiciously.. "Just to be clear," Colton said, "is anybody else in this department working with you?"

Brody shook his head. "No, nobody is."

"Then go sit down," the commander said. "We'll do a full search and wait for the MPs to come and take you to the stockade."

Brody smiled, looked at the commander and said, "You know me. That won't do me for very long."

"But you shouldn't have done this," the commander said. "I don't have any damn choice in the matter."

Brody nodded, then quick as a flash, he lifted his hand and sliced his throat. Blood spurted as he took an instinctive step back. Within seconds he was on his knees, a pool of blood forming around him. "Don't try to stop it," he said. "There's no life for me after this. There was no life for me after Cheryl left anyway." And he collapsed face-first.

The other doctors rushed forward, but the arterial bleeding was too much, too fast and the cut just too deep.

And they couldn't save him.

When Colton stood back up, he walked over to Kate, opened his arms and just held her. "It's all over with now," he said. "It's over—at least here."

"Says you," she said and turned to the commander. "Can I at least count on you to clean house?"

"Yes," he said, "that you can count on. And, while this is all being dealt with," he added, "let's get your shoulder taken care of and get you back to your room. You too, Colton. Looks like that leg needs some attention."

"And here I was hoping for at least a hot bowl of soup," Kate said. "That storm is brutal out there."

"I can handle that too." The commander gave her a smile and patted her gently on her good shoulder. "The next time you come this way," he said, "it will be a whole different story."

"I can't imagine it being much worse," she whispered.

CHAPTER 15

I T SEEMED LIKE forever, but, in less than two hours, Kate was back at Colton's room, after declining the doctor's recommendation for her to stay in the sick bay. The damage to her shoulder had been cleaned up and repaired as much as possible.

"Is it finally bedtime?" she asked with a yawn. Outside she could hear the wind howling and banging against the windows.

"Yes," Colton said, "and hopefully this time you'll sleep for a long time."

"Until the storm is over?"

"It can last for a couple days apparently," he said, "and it doesn't look to me like it'll end anytime soon."

"I guess, if we get to stay and veg out for a day or two, that's okay."

"And the commander did call the hospital, by the way, and George is fine. And so is his family."

"Good," she said. "What about the drug dealer guy?"

"He is still alive, and the police have extra security on him."

"Good enough," she said. She sagged down on Colton's bed and looked up at the top bunk, which looked very difficult to access with a bum shoulder. "Tonight do you mind if I sleep down here?"

"Nope," he said. "Let's get that shirt off you. She had her outer shirt slung over her shoulders. "Did I hear someone say my bag had come in?" Then she noted it on the floor beside her. "Oh, good. Maybe a loose T-shirt is in there that I can wear for the night."

"Or whatever makes you comfortable. But you should decide soon because that painkiller they gave you may hit you at any moment."

With his help, she was completely stripped down, slipped under the covers and tucked up against the wall. "If you want to join me," she said, "I won't argue."

"You need to rest. Besides, I might bump you and hurt your shoulder in the night."

"Maybe," she said, her voice drowsy and sleepy already. "Or I might bump your leg in the night. Or I might not even know you're there."

"I don't know if my ego can handle that," he said jokingly. "And my leg is fine. Besides, we're both on painkillers."

She smiled. "Your ego doesn't need any stroking. It's just fine."

"It's definitely healthy," he said, "but I thought that after we were together last time. Then I just couldn't forget about you. I kept trying, but it didn't work."

"Ditto," she said, yawning. "Maybe we'll have to try again."

"I'm up for it." Pulling the blanket up to her chin, he kissed her gently on the cheek and said, "Go to sleep. We'll talk in the morning." She closed her eyes and sank into a deep sleep. The trouble was, she didn't stay asleep. She surfaced, went under, rolled over, moaned and went under again. Finally she lay here, shaking. "I don't feel so good," she whispered.

"I know," he said, right beside her. She looked up to see Colton lying as far away on the bunk as he could.

"That can't be comfortable," she said, when she realized he was trying to give her space. "Your leg has to be aching, and this sleeping arrangement can't help."

"No," he said, "but watching you toss and turn wasn't good either."

She rolled over and said, "Switch places with me," and then, with her good shoulder down, she tucked up close to him. "This is much better." He chuckled, and the rumble of laughter rolling up his chest made her smile. She stroked his chest and said, "I had just enough sleep that I'm awake now."

"But not enough sleep to keep you awake for long," he said gently, tapping the tip of her nose. "Go back to sleep."

"Maybe I don't want to," she said, sliding her hand across his chest, around his ribs and down onto his belly. His core muscles tightened, and she could feel the ridges of his abs. "You guys are all so damn fit," she muttered.

"You're looking pretty fine yourself."

She smiled. "Not like you guys."

"You don't have to be though," he said, as her hand strayed lower and lower. He grabbed it and said, "Don't go starting something you can't finish."

"I'm just not sure how the logistics would work with our injuries," she said. "I'm not in the greatest of shape right now, but I'm game if you can figure it out."

He murmured, "Maybe you should wait until you're feeling better."

"And yet ..." she said, her voice drifting dreamily. Her hand slid out from under his to glide across his hip to his muscled thighs. "I know just what would make me feel better."

"How do you figure?" he asked, his voice catching in the back of his throat.

"Because some hurts are physical, and some hurts are emotional, and then there are those that are spiritual. Today was a really rough day. And although the physical part of me can't heal as easily, you could do a lot to heal the other two."

He tilted her head and whispered, "Are you sure?"

"Yes," she said, "my soul needs this—and my heart. My body does too. It's just a little more cautious since we're both injured."

"So we'll take it slow," he whispered. And he started by shifting so she lay flat on her back. "I don't want you to move."

"Not happening," she said. "You've got too much of this gorgeous body for me not to touch it."

He lowered his head, his lips leaving a moist trail across her skin as he moved from one breast to lick the nipple before suckling it deeply and then crossing to the next. She twisted beneath him, moaning gently, but he wouldn't let her move much. He held her tight against him as he kissed and stroked, tasting and testing every inch of her until he came to the curve of her ribs, gently caressing, stroking and exploring, making up for the last four years they'd been apart.

She whispered, "I forgot how good you were at this."

"It's not a case of me being good," he said. "It's a case of us being good together."

She moaned as his fingers drifted lower, sliding into the curls at the apex of her thighs. She opened her thighs and whispered, "You know even just this much, to be back in your arms and to know we have this time together is—"

"It's not just tonight," Colton vowed. "I missed you all these years. I kept putting it off, saying it wasn't the right time."

"What makes you think this is the right time?" she asked, but she knew in her heart of hearts she wanted it to be.

"My theory is that fate had a hand in it," he said. "It threw us back together so I could see if I really wanted what I'd lost so long ago."

"And?"

"And the answer is yes," he whispered, as he gently kissed her hip bone. When he shifted to taste the heart of her, his tongue doing crazy magical things, her hips lifted as she moaned, her body twisting under his caress. But he held her hips firm as he deepened the kiss and used his tongue as she'd never known before. When she came apart in his arms, she realized that had been his solution to avoid hurting her. She dragged him up close to her and whispered, "Now your turn."

He shook his head. "You're too injured."

But she wasn't taking no for an answer. She reached up with her thighs wrapped tight around his hips and started to ride the outside of his shaft. He shuddered and shifted so he was in a better position and then slowly entered her.

"Yes, … that's exactly what I want," she said.

"You might get hurt," he said as he gently, ever-so-slowly entered her until he was seated deep inside her. She could feel him holding back. She reached up with her good arm, gently caressing his chest, his neck and his shoulders, her thumb stroking across his lips, and she whispered, "I want this all over again. I want everything you have to give me, so forget about my injury. Give it to me now."

As he lost control, she wrapped her good arm around him to hold herself steady as he drove into her again and again, and unbelievably she could feel her body reacting with the same emotions and passion twisting deeper within her. Arching her body up against him, she cried out yet again. And with great joy and satisfaction she heard him roar above her as he reached his own climax before he slowly collapsed on her good side. When he lay there, gasping for breath, she whispered, "I knew you could figure it out."

He chuckled. "It took a bit, but, yeah, we got it." He kissed her and whispered, "Thank you."

"For what?" she asked.

"For being you and for accepting me being me."

She opened her eyes, wondering where that came from.

"We both needed time apart," he said, "but now that we've had it, we both seem to have rekindled what we want, and, for that, I'm grateful."

She kissed him gently. "Me too," she said. "Now let's not lose the opportunity to work together to have exactly what we both want for tomorrow, not just for tonight."

"No, this isn't just for tonight," he said. "As far as I'm concerned, this is forever." He lay down beside her, gently tucked her up into his arms and held her close.

With a smile and her heart full and her soul so much happier, she closed her eyes and fell back asleep. But this time she knew she'd sleep easy and rest well. Not only did she have everything to make her soul happy and her emotions full but her heart was smiling too.

Her body? Well, that would heal in good time. But it didn't have to heal on its own. Now she could be with Colton and would know they were both reaching for something together.

Forever.

EPILOGUE

A FTER TWO WEEKS in Greenland along with Colton, Troy Landry had finished up the training they had been trying to get done. Once the weather had cleared, their progress had improved rapidly, and now he was on his way back home again. First to Coronado base and then onto a US destroyer. And he was okay with that. He liked to spend as much time out on the water as he could. It was very different being a Navy SEAL on shore versus out on one of the big destroyers. He wasn't sure what the mission was this time, but he was happy to be a part of it, no matter what was happening. He liked excitement; he liked action. But downtime would be nice too.

If any was coming his way.

Back in Coronado, he unpacked, then repacked his gear to be ready when the call came. Just as he moved his bag to the front door before heading down to the pier, he got a phone call.

"Change of orders," Mason said in a clipped voice.

"Okay," Troy said, quite used to having his schedule spin on a dime. "What are we doing instead?"

"Heading up to the coast of Alaska. An oil rig's in trouble. Quite a few workers being rescued right now. A programmer friend of Tesla's called in with an SOS on a suspected sabotage," he said. "She's still on board, as are a few others. Bad storms are coming in."

"So, why are we still talking?" Troy said. "I figured you'd be out front already."

"I am," Mason said, his laugh dark. "I was hoping you're on your way out to the pier."

With the phone still in his hand, Troy took one last look around, shut off the lights, grabbed his bag and opened his front door. Locking it, he said, "I'm coming down the hallway toward you."

"Good thing," Mason said. "This one looks bad."

"How many teams?"

"One six-man team," Mason said.

Before they were done talking, Troy was out front, storing his duffel bag into the back of the navy jeep before taking the last vacant spot in the back seat. Lots of faces he knew and a couple he didn't. He just smiled and said, "Good to go." He slammed the door shut even as Mason pulled away from the curb. "Are we going incognito or is this with full military backing?"

"Always military backing," Axel said from the front of the truck. "Just, in this case, we're also talking a little bit of stealth."

"Great," Troy said. "And what's our cover?"

"Two of us are part of the oil company, heading onto the rig itself," Mason said, "and two will be on a nearby destroyer and will be coming in from the ocean. We'll let them onto the rig, and they will be our eyes and ears in the shadows."

"Oh, now that's an interesting way to handle it," Troy said. "And the other two?"

Mason shot him a look through the rearview mirror. "You and Axel will go on as deckhands."

"Why are we new deckhands, if they're trying to get everybody off because the oil rig is in danger?"

"Because they still need somebody to stay on board and hopefully stabilize it."

"Surely they're not taking the entire crew off, are they?"

"They're trying to," Mason said. "Nelson here and I will go in as part of the company. And unfortunately one of the actual company board members is coming with us."

"Unfortunately?"

"It's never a good idea to have civilians involved," he said.

Troy sat back and nodded, agreeing fully. This started to sound like an interesting mission. "Loss of life?"

"They're still checking. Four people are missing."

"But not confirmed dead?"

Axel shook his head, as he twisted around to look at him. "No, none confirmed yet. Several were fished out of the arctic water already."

"What's it take? About twelve minutes for hypothermia up there?"

"If you're lucky," he said. "An arctic front is heading down, so the weather'll get vicious."

"My favorite kind of mission then," Troy said with a laugh. "Maximum danger, potential for betrayal, chances of not coming home—all good." He grinned, and the others laughed. Because, just like him, they'd all been there before. And, just like him, so far they'd been lucky and made it home. But, just like him, they all knew many who hadn't. Being part of the oil crew suited Troy just fine. He'd actually done a stint up on the oil rigs himself when he was eighteen, which may be why he'd been tagged for this. He looked over at Axel. "You ever been on a rig before?"

"Yeah," Axel said. "A couple times."

Troy wasn't at all surprised at that. The men on this team had a wide and varied set of experiences. When they pulled into the base airport, without talking they headed for the plane already refueling.

One of the pilots stood there, glaring at them. "You're late," he said.

Troy lifted an eyebrow.

By the time they made the switch to a connecting flight to head to Alaska and then eventually landed on the destroyer, Troy would be tired and ready for either action or a break. This hurry-up-and-wait scenario was driving him crazy. They'd done as much research as they could, but, so far, it looked like it could be an accident, sabotage or somebody trying to make it look like sabotage to hide something else. He'd seen way too much betrayal in his life to not consider that as an option.

After several hours on the destroyer, they were called up on deck to climb into the helicopter heading to the oil rig platform. He and Axel were in oil-rig uniforms but were fully armed inside the coveralls and heavy jackets. Mason was there in a heavy parka, but he wore a suit, as was the stranger standing with them, looking uncomfortable. Presumably the board member.

Mason introduced them. "This is Gregor Stanovich, one of the board members, and the one who looks after this particular rig." Mason motioned everybody toward the chopper.

Troy studied Gregor carefully and concluded he definitely looked like the paper-pushing kind. But Troy had been deceived before. He glanced at Axel to see him eyeing the stranger with the same harsh eye.

Not everybody was as quick to do this kind of work as they were. And it wasn't that Gregor should be doing it. Everybody had a place in this world to do their own thing, but it was also important to know what capabilities somebody had.

By insisting on going into this nightmare, Gregor was putting himself in the midst of the fire. And that just meant Troy and his team would have to keep an eye on him, in case things went south.

Civilians tended not to listen; they tended to underestimate the danger, and they just didn't see the traps as they headed toward them. Troy could only hope this was a case of a simple accident, but there was a reason his team had been called in. And it was rarely for a simple accident. Too often a "simple accident" ended up being something far worse.

From the helicopter, Troy watched the destroyer come into view below them. There was no sign of the oil rig in the distance. Which meant they still had quite a distance to go. He looked at Axel. "I wonder how close the destroyer is planning on getting."

Axel nodded. "Nobody can handle the frigid water, no matter what kind of protective gear they've got."

"Do we have a submersible down there?"

Axel shot him half a glance and said, "What do you think?"

"Do we know if it's safe to land?" They both kept their voices low, looking out the window at the oil rig. There might have been an accident, but Troy wasn't seeing anything to indicate just what that had been. "They said something about an explosion, some part of the rig collapsing and some fire." He motioned down below. "I'm not seeing evidence of that."

"It was inside, I believe," Axel said, but his look was hard as he studied the rig they approached. "Stay alive," he muttered.

Troy's reaction was instinctive. "Always."

This concludes Book 23 of SEALs of Honor: Colton.

Read about Troy: SEALs of Honor, Book 24

SEALS OF HONOR: TROY BOOK 24

When a friend of Tesla's sends out an SOS on the lowdown on an oil rig in trouble, Troy has a good idea what he's getting into. As far as he is concerned, the maximum danger, the potential for betrayal, and the chances of not coming home sounded like the right kind of job for him.

After all, he lived alone. So going into these situations with no family to worry about him made him the ideal candidate—until he meets someone at the oil rig who suddenly makes him see his future in a different life.

Berkley knew something dangerous was going on. No way this oil rig hadn't been sabotaged. She'd requested to remain with the skeleton crew until her help arrived. And was surprised at the size of the team that showed up to assist her.

Who knew it would take all of them to get to the bottom of this mess and to keep them alive, as human nature and Mother Nature combined to take them all out.

Find Book 24 here!
To find out more visit Dale Mayer's website.
http://smarturl.it/DMSTroy

Author's Note

Thank you for reading Colton: SEALs of Honor, Book 23! If you enjoyed the book, please take a moment and leave a short review.

Dear reader,

I love to hear from readers, and you can contact me at my website: www.dalemayer.com or at my Facebook author page. To be informed of new releases and special offers, sign up for my newsletter or follow me on BookBub. And if you are interested in joining Dale Mayer's Reader Group, here is the Facebook sign up page.
https://smarturl.it/DaleMayerFBGroup

Cheers,
Dale Mayer

COMPLIMENTARY DOWNLOAD

DOWNLOAD a *complimentary* copy of TUESDAY'S CHILD? Just tell me where to send it!

http://dalemayer.com/starterlibrarytc/

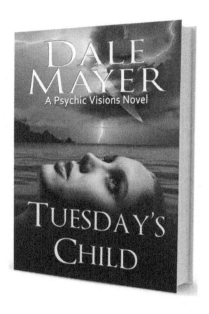

About the Author

Dale Mayer is a USA Today bestselling author best known for her Psychic Visions and Family Blood Ties series. Her contemporary romances are raw and full of passion and emotion (Second Chances, SKIN), her thrillers will keep you guessing (By Death series), and her romantic comedies will keep you giggling (It's a Dog's Life and Charmin Marvin Romantic Comedy series).

She honors the stories that come to her – and some of them are crazy and break all the rules and cross multiple genres!

To go with her fiction, she also writes nonfiction in many different fields with books available on resume writing, companion gardening and the US mortgage system. She has recently published her Career Essentials Series. All her books are available in print and ebook format.

Connect with Dale Mayer Online

Dale's Website – www.dalemayer.com
Facebook Personal – https://smarturl.it/DaleMayer
Instagram – https://smarturl.it/DaleMayerInstagram
BookBub – https://smarturl.it/DaleMayerBookbub
Facebook Fan Page – https://smarturl.it/DaleMayerFBFanPage
Goodreads – https://smarturl.it/DaleMayerGoodreads

Also by Dale Mayer

Published Adult Books:

Hathaway House
Aaron, Book 1
Brock, Book 2
Cole, Book 3
Denton, Book 4
Elliot, Book 5
Finn, Book 6
Gregory, Book 7
Heath, Book 8
Iain, Book 9

The K9 Files
Ethan, Book 1
Pierce, Book 2
Zane, Book 3
Blaze, Book 4
Lucas, Book 5
Parker, Book 6
Carter, Book 7

Lovely Lethal Gardens
Arsenic in the Azaleas, Book 1
Bones in the Begonias, Book 2
Corpse in the Carnations, Book 3

Daggers in the Dahlias, Book 4
Evidence in the Echinacea, Book 5
Footprints in the Ferns, Book 6
Gun in the Gardenias, Book 7
Handcuffs in the Heather, Book 8
Ice Pick in the Ivy, Book 9

Psychic Vision Series
Tuesday's Child
Hide 'n Go Seek
Maddy's Floor
Garden of Sorrow
Knock Knock...
Rare Find
Eyes to the Soul
Now You See Her
Shattered
Into the Abyss
Seeds of Malice
Eye of the Falcon
Itsy-Bitsy Spider
Unmasked
Deep Beneath
From the Ashes
Stroke of Death
Psychic Visions Books 1–3
Psychic Visions Books 4–6
Psychic Visions Books 7–9

By Death Series
Touched by Death
Haunted by Death

Chilled by Death
By Death Books 1–3

Broken Protocols – Romantic Comedy Series
Cat's Meow
Cat's Pajamas
Cat's Cradle
Cat's Claus
Broken Protocols 1-4

Broken and... Mending
Skin
Scars
Scales (of Justice)
Broken but… Mending 1-3

Glory
Genesis
Tori
Celeste
Glory Trilogy

Biker Blues
Morgan: Biker Blues, Volume 1
Cash: Biker Blues, Volume 2

SEALs of Honor
Mason: SEALs of Honor, Book 1
Hawk: SEALs of Honor, Book 2
Dane: SEALs of Honor, Book 3
Swede: SEALs of Honor, Book 4
Shadow: SEALs of Honor, Book 5
Cooper: SEALs of Honor, Book 6

Markus: SEALs of Honor, Book 7
Evan: SEALs of Honor, Book 8
Mason's Wish: SEALs of Honor, Book 9
Chase: SEALs of Honor, Book 10
Brett: SEALs of Honor, Book 11
Devlin: SEALs of Honor, Book 12
Easton: SEALs of Honor, Book 13
Ryder: SEALs of Honor, Book 14
Macklin: SEALs of Honor, Book 15
Corey: SEALs of Honor, Book 16
Warrick: SEALs of Honor, Book 17
Tanner: SEALs of Honor, Book 18
Jackson: SEALs of Honor, Book 19
Kanen: SEALs of Honor, Book 20
Nelson: SEALs of Honor, Book 21
Taylor: SEALs of Honor, Book 22
Colton: SEALs of Honor, Book 23
Troy: SEALs of Honor, Book 24
SEALs of Honor, Books 1–3
SEALs of Honor, Books 4–6
SEALs of Honor, Books 7–10
SEALs of Honor, Books 11–13
SEALs of Honor, Books 14–16
SEALs of Honor, Books 17–19

Heroes for Hire

Levi's Legend: Heroes for Hire, Book 1
Stone's Surrender: Heroes for Hire, Book 2
Merk's Mistake: Heroes for Hire, Book 3
Rhodes's Reward: Heroes for Hire, Book 4
Flynn's Firecracker: Heroes for Hire, Book 5
Logan's Light: Heroes for Hire, Book 6

Harrison's Heart: Heroes for Hire, Book 7
Saul's Sweetheart: Heroes for Hire, Book 8
Dakota's Delight: Heroes for Hire, Book 9
Michael's Mercy (Part of Sleeper SEAL Series)
Tyson's Treasure: Heroes for Hire, Book 10
Jace's Jewel: Heroes for Hire, Book 11
Rory's Rose: Heroes for Hire, Book 12
Brandon's Bliss: Heroes for Hire, Book 13
Liam's Lily: Heroes for Hire, Book 14
North's Nikki: Heroes for Hire, Book 15
Anders's Angel: Heroes for Hire, Book 16
Reyes's Raina: Heroes for Hire, Book 17
Dezi's Diamond: Heroes for Hire, Book 18
Vince's Vixen: Heroes for Hire, Book 19
Ice's Icing: Heroes for Hire, Book 20
Johan's Joy: Heroes for Hire, Book 21
Heroes for Hire, Books 1–3
Heroes for Hire, Books 4–6
Heroes for Hire, Books 7–9
Heroes for Hire, Books 10–12
Heroes for Hire, Books 13–15

SEALs of Steel
Badger: SEALs of Steel, Book 1
Erick: SEALs of Steel, Book 2
Cade: SEALs of Steel, Book 3
Talon: SEALs of Steel, Book 4
Laszlo: SEALs of Steel, Book 5
Geir: SEALs of Steel, Book 6
Jager: SEALs of Steel, Book 7
The Final Reveal: SEALs of Steel, Book 8
SEALs of Steel, Books 1–4

SEALs of Steel, Books 5–8
SEALs of Steel, Books 1–8

The Mavericks

Kerrick, Book 1
Griffin, Book 2
Jax, Book 3
Beau, Book 4
Asher, Book 5
Ryker, Book 6
Miles, Book 7
Nico, Book 8
Keane, Book 9
Lennox, Book 10
Gavin, Book 11
Shane, Book 12

Bullard's Battle Series

Ryland's Reach, Book 1
Cain's Cross, Book 2
Eton's Escape, Book 3
Garret's Gambit, Book 4
Kano's Keep, Book 5
Fallon's Flaw, Book 6
Quinn's Quest, Book 7
Bullard's Beauty, Book 8

Collections

Dare to Be You…
Dare to Love…
Dare to be Strong…
RomanceX3

Standalone Novellas
It's a Dog's Life
Riana's Revenge
Second Chances

Published Young Adult Books:

Family Blood Ties Series
Vampire in Denial
Vampire in Distress
Vampire in Design
Vampire in Deceit
Vampire in Defiance
Vampire in Conflict
Vampire in Chaos
Vampire in Crisis
Vampire in Control
Vampire in Charge
Family Blood Ties Set 1–3
Family Blood Ties Set 1–5
Family Blood Ties Set 4–6
Family Blood Ties Set 7–9
Sian's Solution, A Family Blood Ties Series Prequel
    Novelette

Design series
Dangerous Designs
Deadly Designs
Darkest Designs
Design Series Trilogy

Standalone
In Cassie's Corner
Gem Stone (a Gemma Stone Mystery)
Time Thieves

Published Non-Fiction Books:

Career Essentials
Career Essentials: The Résumé
Career Essentials: The Cover Letter
Career Essentials: The Interview
Career Essentials: 3 in 1